REDUCTION

Reduction

This is a work of fiction. All names, characters, places, and events are creations of the author's imagination. Any resemblance to any actual person, living or dead, is purely coincidental.

Copyright © 2017 by Brian Cheatham
All rights reserved.

Printed by CreateSpace, an Amazon.com Company

ISBN 978-1-546-93092-1

Available from Amazon.com, CreateSpace.com, and other retail outlets.

Second Edition October 2017

Reduction

Special thanks to Tina, Dorothy, and Jay whose support and encouragement made this book possible.

Follow me online at
briancheatham.net

Special Thanks to Gino Santa Maria and
Pond5.com for the cover photo.

To Janice,
Welcome to Reduction!
I hope you enjoy the antics of
Mark Hime & the others.
Brian

Reduction

Reduction

by

Brian Cheatham

Chapter 1

Mark Himes closed the door on the five axis Fanuc CNC machine and started the machining process. In a couple of hours the block of raw aluminum would be a finely turned component in a line-side assembly fixture. In the 14 years that Himes had worked as a machinist he never seemed to be amazed by how much technology had revolutionized his line of work. The tool room of the plant that he worked in was cluttered with equipment from decades of procurement. From the simplest brake press to this behemoth before him, the list of machinery spanned more years than he had been alive.

"Meeting in 30 minutes. Don't be late," Joey Davis called over his shoulder as Himes made a note on his project list. He had known Davis for most of his time in the tool room and the two had become good friends early on. Davis was always quick with a joke or snappy comment, but rarely socialized outside of work.

"Oh, don't worry. I wouldn't miss it for the world. After all, today's the day they are going to name me as president of this place."

Davis laughed, "And your first change is to give me a raise and a company car, right?"

"Absolutely. Five cents an hour and the best Yugo I can find." he quipped. Himes took a quick peek at the Fanuc and checked his list to see what the next item was. He might have time to get started on a small project before having to retrieve his component from the massive machine. He turned to the workbench beside his tool box and reached in the inbox on the corner for a small set of prints. Flipping to a fresh sheet in his notepad he began to make a material list of all the raw stock needed to build the small fixture.

Reduction

After a few minutes the door to the office swung open and the tool and die supervisor shouted down to the machine shop floor.

"Staff meeting in five minutes! Drop what you're doing and head to the shipping docks!"

Almost as if a master switch had been flipped, the brakes and drill presses all became silent except for the monstrous computer controlled Fanuc which still busied itself with Himes' program. Slowly the tool room emptied of staff as each locked their tool boxes and made their way toward the shipping docks in the center section of the massive plant.

When they arrived the room, despite its size, was packed from wall to wall with employees from all sections of the facility, save one corner where the plant managers and executives stood on either side of a portable rostrum. Cables leading out from either side traced their way across the floor and up spindly metal legs to the backs of speakers to help make sure

Reduction

the message presented was loud and clear.

In the days prior, rumors had flown from one extreme to another about the nature of the meeting. The last time that an assembly like this had been called was just before contract negotiations and that had cost the employees a very comfortable benefits package and some significant loss of pay on the production rated assembly lines. The only constant among the rumors was that the outcome would not be good.

After several minutes waiting for the last stragglers to squeeze in, the VP of operations stepped up to the microphone and produced a small handful of index cards.

"Good afternoon, ladies and gentlemen. I want to first thank all of you for taking the time to be here. I know it can be disruptive to your routines to have to drop what you are working on and, for those who still work in our piece work areas, can be equally disruptive to your paychecks.

"If you will bear with me for a moment, I have been asked to review the year to date profit and loss figures with you before I turn the mic over to the President for his announcement."

"Uh oh," Davis mumbled in Himes' direction, "someone's getting laid off. They never talk money unless they intend to 'save' some for the company."

Himes didn't say anything, but the thought was already there. He had worked here long enough to know that the executives always justified layoffs and cutbacks with the facts and figures from sales and market share, but it always meant that the workload increased while the manpower decreased. Over the years it had become traditional to have massive hiring sprees followed by layoffs to weed out the ones who didn't perform. Then the ones that were left were put on extended shifts to build inventory so they could be laid off, usually just before the holidays. In so doing, the company didn't have to pay as much in holiday pay, but still got enough product stockpiled to maintain shipments with only a skeleton crew at the plant. It was an odd way of doing business, but at this point it was more of a tradition than a business plan anyway.

This meeting felt different, though. There had been no hiring spree and no increase in production anywhere. By all accounts the inventory levels were already maxed out and had been maintained at capacity for a number of weeks. Himes' mind drifted briefly through other possibilities for the conference, but nothing really seemed to make any more sense. When the President took the mic, his attention quickly returned to the corner of the room.

"Thank you, Jim," he began. The look on his face was stern and almost pale. Whatever he was about to say clearly made the veteran businessman uncomfortable. As he stood at the rostrum, his expression changed subtly from that of a wizened professional to more of a caring grandfather. He rested his arms across the top of the rostrum and scanned the crowd, gathering his thoughts before speaking.

"Boys and girls, it's been my pleasure to have worked with you all for the past 23 years. Some of you I consider to be, well, almost like family. Others, I haven't had the honor of properly meeting. That's the way the world works when you're in my position," he shifted his weight and straightened his stance, pushing both hands into his pockets.

"Another thing that I have to deal with in my world is the communication of news, good or bad, as it pertains to you...and me. Today I have asked everyone to gather here for news that will impact everyone here.

Reduction

"A few months ago I was notified that the board of directors had been looking into some extreme cost saving measures in order to gain market share without having to increase operating costs. Now, I can tell that some of you already see where this is going, but let me finish.

"The board reached a decision earlier this week and, despite numerous objections, they have declared it final. Effective the 18th of next month, production operations at this facility will stop and the biggest majority of us will be out of a job."

He paused for a second to allow the magnitude of the announcement sink in before continuing with the details. The murmur growing in the crowd forced the executive to raise his voice a bit to regain control of the moment.

"Let me continue, please. The physical building will be used, at least temporarily, as a warehouse and distribution center. Some of you will remain here to staff that operation, but remember that it may only be temporary. We will also maintain a skeleton crew for rework until that function can be relocated. To support these functions a small administrative staff will be necessary as will a small maintenance crew. Some will be given the opportunity to accompany equipment to the new location and assist with setup and training functions. These positions are voluntary and temporary. Once the new guys can stand on their own two feet you will be out of a job."

"Where, exactly, is this new location anyway?" The faceless voice echoed over the crowd.

"Manufacturing and assembly operations are moving to Mexico. Tool and die operations are being outsourced to China and Mexico and the paint lines are being eliminated altogether in favor of pre-painted coils. I don't suppose there are many in this group that are surprised by that information. It seems that the board has decided to jump on the bandwagon with everyone else and help add to the local unemployment. Details of all the changes will be posted on bulletin boards throughout the plant by the end of the day.

"Now, for the good news," he continued, "The company has decided that since they are cutting so many positions in such a short time that they need to make amends in some way. Everyone who will be losing their job will be given a few options to help ease the pain. Those of us who are close to retirement age will be offered a retirement package based on what we could have gotten at full term. Bear in mind that this will not be what you would get if you could have stayed to draw your full retirement funds, but it will be a percentage.

"Everyone else will be offered assistance in unemployment filing and job placement for a period of six months after the close of regular operations.

Reduction

After that, you're on your own. Personally, I suggest you take full advantage of everything they offer." He scanned the crowd, again letting the words sink in.

"What happens to you and the management?" Another faceless voice called out.

"Some of us have decided to ride the relocation out and move to the Mexico facility. Others have decided to cut ties and start looking elsewhere immediately. As for me, well, I can't lie, folks. I'm pretty pissed off about the whole deal. I don't think it's right and I've told the board how I feel. I'm too old to go find a job somewhere else and too stuck in my ways to learn anything new, so I've decided to take the package they've offered and make do.

"I know it's going to be difficult to focus on your daily tasks after this bombshell. I have been pretty distracted myself trying to figure out the best way to pass the word along to you. If you have questions, which I'm sure most of you do, my door is open. At this time I'll let you get back to work because, as of right now, we still have work to do and we won't get paid without doing it. I'd suggest that if you have the opportunity to make a dollar here you make the very most of it in the time you have available. Thank you again for your time."

With that the older gentleman stepped away from the microphone and began working his way toward the large doorway back into the main area of the plant. The crowd moved like a stunned amoeba, slowly drifting back toward the same door and then splitting off toward various aisles and departments. A few stood in small groups discussing the unwelcome news that had just been thrust upon them. Still, others already had cell phones in hand, frantically texting and dialing to pass the word along to friends and family members.

Reduction

Back in the tool room Himes checked in on the progress of the CNC, estimating another 45 minutes or so until the program completed. As he turned around he noticed Davis standing by his workbench looking somewhat lost and confused. Himes made his way over to Davis' work area and struck up a conversation.

"Bombshell, huh?"

"Yeah. No kidding."

"You OK? You look sort of lost, man."

"Hmm? Oh, yeah. It's just that I don't know where I'm gonna go, you know? I mean, jobs around here are scarce and I'm not exactly set up for a commute. I never figured on losing my job after finally getting some seniority, so I never worried much about investing or saving. Man, I was going to retire from this place."

"Yeah, I understand," Himes said, now thinking even more about his own situation. He and

Reduction

Angie had saved up a few dollars for an emergency fund, but it had never grown and they had both tapped into it from time to time for life's little "emergencies" that crept up. The only other savings they had were supposed to be for the kids college funds and they were supposed to be inaccessible. They would be able to keep current on bills with her income as an administrative assistant, but that didn't leave o lot of room for groceries, clothes, or much else. That would be problematic since the kids were still growing and clothes were a struggle even with two checks coming in.

That evening after work he stopped by the first convenience store he passed and picked up a copy of the latest newspaper. He and Angie would have to get a plan together quickly and stick to it.

As soon as he walked in the door she could tell something was wrong. You can't be married to someone for 15 years and not learn to read expressions. She waited for him to get settled and give him the chance to fill her in on the details. If it was urgent he would have said something as soon as he opened the door. No sense in pressing the issue before he was ready to talk about it.

"How was your day?" He finally asked, slipping out of his work boots and reaching for the paper.

"Fine. We have a group coming in from corporate Thursday, so everyone is getting nervous, wanting to make sure everything looks like it should and works like it's supposed to." She paused for a moment before returning the query, "How was yours?"

Himes smiled sheepishly and folded the paper in his lap. As he turned to face her, she handed him a glass of iced tea and took a seat in the chair to his right.

Reduction

"Fine. Got quite a few things knocked off my list today." He took a long sip from his glass, reading the anticipation on her face, "Had a meeting today. Company-wide. Looks like there's going to be some big changes at the factory."

"Good changes, I hope?"

"Good for Mexico. Not so good for us. They've decided to move the production and assembly to Mexico. That means that all the supporting departments will be outsourced as well. Looks like I'll be out of a job in a few weeks."

"They're shutting everything down?"

"No, they plan on keeping the building for a distribution center until they can find a better place."

"Can you transfer to another department or anything? Is there any way you can use your seniority to pull some strings and keep a check coming in?"

"I already thought of that. The problem is that they already have a full staff doing those jobs that don't need to be trained. It all depends on how many of them want to stay after the rest of the plant is gone as to how many positions may be open. The reality of it is that I need to keep looking, just to be on the safe side."

They talked off and on for the rest of the evening and decided that Angie would start learning how to coupon while Mark would spend extra time hunting and fishing to offset grocery costs. In the meantime he would take advantage of every offer of assistance from the company for placement and unemployment. Additionally, Mark maintained a small machine shop out back of the house for hobbies and the occasional side job.

Thursday evening he phoned his long time friend and hunting buddy, John Thompson, to meet him at the range. Himes needed to zero his hunting rifle for the fast approaching deer season and having an extra pair of eyes to man the spotting scope was always convenient. Plus, Thompson had always been a close confidant and trusted friend; someone good to bounce ideas off of and get feedback from.

Saturday morning rolled around and Himes loaded his rifle, ammunition, spotting scope, and a portable bench into the truck, grabbed a small lunch bag with sandwiches and drinks, kissed his wife, and headed for the range. On the floor of the truck sat a small, black nylon bag. Inside was Himes .45 ACP and some extra magazines in case they had the chance for some extra trigger time on one of the pistol ranges.

Being a police officer, Thompson always liked to spend extra time on the range whenever he could, especially when it involved practice with a sidearm. The department didn't typically send anyone for additional training outside of what was provided at the academy and most officers didn't care to put the time and money aside for training on their own either.

Reduction

The department would reimburse their expenses, but most didn't like the hassle of more paperwork in a job that already overwhelmed every free moment with logs and reports.

By the time Himes arrived at the range Thompson's Jeep was already there. He unloaded his gear and dropped it at the bench on the 50 yard range. They would set up targets at 25 yards initially to sight in and then move over to the 100 yard range to verify. Thompson set up the target stand while Himes prepared his bench rest and chair at the firing line table.

"How's that look to you?" Thompson called back to the table.

"Looks good. Let's see how far off this thing is from last season."

Thompson strode back to the shelter where Himes was already pulling the scoped .30-06 from its case.

"You bump the scope?"

"No, but I'm shooting some new ammo this time around and I need to double check it for zero. I'd hate to miss supper because of something as stupid as not checking when I have the chance." Himes settled into the chair and rested the fore end of the rifle in the fork of the rest, then slipped his eye and ear protection on. Thompson did likewise and scooted up to the spotting scope.

"Ready?"

"Send it."

Himes' first three shot group was slightly to the right of center and covered an area one half of an inch across.

"Tight group, but you need to adjust left about an inch."

Himes turned the windage knob and loaded three more rounds into the magazine, then snuggled up to the rifle again. The three follow-up shots were

Reduction

dead center and, like before, all three holes touched. Time to adjust for elevation.

Settling behind the scope again, Himes shot his third group an inch and a half below center. The rifle was now set to zero at 100 yards. He opened the bolt after the last shot and flipped the smoking case out, onto the table then looked at his spotter and smiled.

"I can't believe how simple you make that look," Thompson started, "The last time I sighted in a rifle it took me three boxes of ammo and a couple of hours."

"Well, if you do it enough it becomes second nature, I guess." Himes commented. "This time it has a whole new level of importance."

He told his friend about the changes at the plant and the assistance they were offering as part of the severance packages. How he and his wife had agreed to offset expenses by hunting and fishing more to put food on the table and how he had been scouring the wanted papers and job sites, with little out there.

Thompson considered his friends position and then asked, "How long have you got before they close your department?"

"About three more weeks. Got any suggestions?"

"Not really. You know, it's a shame you're so old."

"Thanks. It's a shame you're so friggin' ugly."

Thompson couldn't help but laugh. "No, no, I didn't mean it like that. I meant that if you were a few years younger you could attend the academy and join the department. We are always looking for new officers and you've got a pretty good head on your shoulders. I think you would make a good cop. Plus, the way you shoot you could probably slip into a sniper position easily."

Reduction

"Well, if a frog had wings...."

"Ha! Yeah, that's right. I tell you what, I'll keep my eyes and ears open and if I find anything I'll let you know. Sometimes we meet people on patrol that have info on more than just crime."

The next three weeks passed with increasing tension at the plant and a couple of deer in the freezer at the Himes house. Angie had been hard at work working the couponing angle at every opportunity and they had actually been able to stock up on a number of canned goods and hygiene products as well as detergents and paper goods.

On the last day of production at the plant, Mark took a few minutes to meet with the career counselors that the company had brought in. They had him fill out several forms and answer a questionnaire, then scheduled him for some skills tests to make him more appealing to potential employers. They helped him file for unemployment insurance benefits and gave him an information packet containing dozens of job search sites online, including many he had never heard of.

At the end of the day he shook hands with everyone in the department and made his way to the workstation that his tools had called home for so many years. He locked up his tool box and gave one last look around before heading to the time clock. As he headed out the main gate he noticed an unusual bottleneck at the guard house. He started his truck and dropped in line, waiting to pass through the checkpoint for the last time. As he finally approached the gate he realized what the hold up had been. There, standing at the window, was the president of the company. Shaking each employee's hand and thanking them for their service.

Mark pulled up and rolled his window down as he slowed to a stop.

"Mark, I just wanted to say, 'thanks' for all your years of hard work. I wish I could say more."

"Thank you, sir. We'll manage. You take care now and maybe I'll see you around."

"Maybe," the older man smiled, "You just never know where the road will take you."

Over the next several weeks Himes poured over the ads and job postings, making call after call and submitting applications and resumes until it became as second nature to him as sighting in a rifle. He had set up a folder in his home computer dedicated to job hunting that contained various formatted copies of his resume, cover letters, and other reference materials and documents that he found useful. Angie would take time to scan the pages as well and often helped him double check listings for commute times and salaries to make sure the pay for the job was worth the drive.

Reduction

The income from his unemployment check helped and they were actually scraping by, albeit barely. From time to time he would pick up a small job doing some machine work, which helped keep his mind off the more stressful days and his skills sharp. Regardless, he hated having to rely on anyone for help, especially what he considered charity. Still, finding gainful employment was becoming such a frustrating effort that he had even widened the search to include jobs he didn't really want, but that he could do if he had to. He and Angie both knew how much he had to take home to maintain their cost of living, so Mark had begun to search more by salary range than any other parameter.

Of the dozens of job submissions he had put forth he had only had a small percentage of them to call or email him back. Of those the biggest majority were form rejections. Not a single one was a follow up for an interview.

Reduction

Before long it was time for his unemployment benefits to roll over into the extension fund authorized by the government. The thought of being out of work so long left a pang of nausea in his stomach. Himes had been unemployed for six months with no sign of steady work in the near future. The extension just seemed to drive that fact home even harder.

One Wednesday evening, just before dinner, Mark's phone rang. He picked up and recognized the number to be John Thompson's. Maybe John had stumbled on a job somewhere and was calling to let him know the details. Mark quickly answered with a lilt in his voice.

"Hey, man, what's up?"

"Not much. How's everything going with you?"

"Same old same old. Still looking at the want ads. You hear anything anywhere?"

Reduction

"Well, maybe. I want to talk to you about something, but I don't want to do it over the phone. Could I interest you in a range day Saturday?"

Mark's first instinct was that it was a somewhat odd request, but then it could be that the job wasn't common knowledge and John could be a bit paranoid about things. Maybe he was just trying to make sure that only Mark found out about it. After all, people still eavesdropped on phone conversations, didn't they?

"Yeah, I can do that. What time and what are you shooting?"

"Let's say 10:00 and bring whatever you want. I need to brush up on my scattergun, but don't let that influence you. Bring whatever you need to work on."

"Sounds good. I'll see you then," Mark paused for a second, "John?"

"Yeah?"

"Is this something that you're sure I'll be able to do?"

"Able? No doubt. Willing is the question. We'll talk about it Saturday. Until then, this stays between you and me, OK?"

"Sure. I'll see you Saturday."

The two friends hung up and Mark sat for a minute, his mind racing through the possible job opportunities that John might have come across.

"Willing?" Himes thought, *"What could he have meant by 'willing?' At this point I'm willing to flip burgers or wash cars for the right money."*

"Who was that, honey?" Angie's sudden question startled him. He hadn't realized she was within earshot.

"John. He wants to head to the range Saturday and run shotguns."

"Oh. I was hoping it was a recruiter. You going to meet him, then?"

Reduction

"Yeah, I could use the stress relief. And, who knows, maybe he's stumbled on someone needing a job filled."

"Oh, wouldn't that be nice?"

Himes spent the rest of the evening in an almost daydream state wondering what he would find out that weekend.

Saturday morning finally came and Mark busied himself with loading gear for his meeting with John. His range bag carried his trusty .45 and extra magazines, plus 50 rounds of 12 gauge 00 buck and 2 boxes of pheasant loads in case they shot against the steel popper targets. Then he stuffed in his eye and ear protection and a couple of magazines for his AR-15. John always liked to run the tactical courses and Mark had to admit they could be fun. They ran them often enough that he bought the Sabre Defense just for that reason. He had never really used his carbine for hunting, he preferred a larger caliber round for that, but it was a handy size and he often considered making it a "truck gun."

He grabbed his AR in one hand and his range bag in the other and proceeded to the truck where the Remington 1100 already rested in its Pelican case. On the way out he took note of both kids seemingly glued to the TV in the family room. He couldn't help but think of how lucky he really was. That, despite his current situation, he had truly been blessed to have such a wonderful family. He knew that they would do anything for him, and in return, he knew that he would do the same for them. That thought brought him back to the conversation with John and made him wonder again what he might be doing before long.

Mark rolled up to the shooting range and, as usual, there sat John's Jeep. This time Thompson sat in it instead of already being on the firing line.

Apparently he had only beaten Mark by a few minutes.

"Howdy," Mark called to his friend, "Been waiting long?"

"Nope. Just got here myself. What did you bring to play with today?"

"Remington 1100, AR-15, and, of course, the Colt. You?"

"Ah, fun stuff. I brought my AR, Glock, and the 870. Are you ready to get started?"

"Of course! I've been looking forward to today since you called the other night. Can you give me any details?"

"Whoa, there," Thompson smiled, "Let's get set up first. There's plenty of time for that."

The pair started off as John had wanted, with the shotguns. They began with pepper poppers situated to simulate multiple person threats at close range, moving the steel reactive targets from time to time to make the setup more challenging, or realistic, or just downright difficult. Each time Mark ran the course John would offer constructive criticism on his exposure, stance, speed, or some other detail to make him run faster, smoother, safer, or more accurate.

Mark didn't mind the pointers at all, but he couldn't help but think that John was acting a bit more like an instructor than usual.

"You know, that 1100 of yours would be really nice with, say, a 20" barrel and a mag tube extension. That would make it a lot quicker handling shotgun and give you more capacity for follow-up shots." John commented after Mark's latest run.

"Yeah, but that sort of defeats the purpose of a 'hunting' shotgun, don't you think?"

"I guess that all depends on what you're hunting."

John's flat tone and serious expression didn't go unnoticed. Himes laid the shotgun across the table at the support structure and pulled up a seat.

"So, tell me about this wonderful job opportunity you have for me."

Thompson propped his tactical model Remington 870 against the wall of the small shelter they were in and also pulled a chair over.

"You know Chief Dahlgren, right?"

"Sure. I mean, I don't know him personally, but I know who you're talking about."

"Yeah, well, he and I were talking a few days ago about how crime was on the increase what with the economy being in the toilet and all and so many being unemployed. Anyway, I brought your situation into the conversation to see if there was anything you could do for the department, possibly some kind of support role or administrative position."

"Okay. What did he say?"

"Well, to be blunt, he said that the best thing anyone could do for the department was to take out some of the bigger criminal elements that we just can't seem to lock up."

"So, you're asking me to be an officer? I thought I was too old to attend the academy."

"No, not an officer," Thompson started, "more like...a hit man."

"What? Man, I thought you were serious! Here you get my hopes up about a job and pull off a joke like that. You ought to be ashamed, getting me all excited."

"No joke, Mark." The expression on Thompson's face was calm and serious, "Dahlgren has become pretty frustrated over the past few years with the way the system works, or doesn't, depending on where you stand. There are people out there that we *know* are doing bad things, heinous things, and we can't get the hard evidence to arrest, let alone convict them. They have networks of people that won't turn on them so we can't get witnesses or testimony from them either."

"But, surely you could arrest on probable cause or something, couldn't you? I mean if you know what they're doing it should be easy to pick them up, right?"

"It should be, but it's not that simple anymore. With the cash they have on hand they can pretty much buy loyalty, and if they can't they can buy a good lawyer with morals as bad as theirs. The ones that we do actually catch and take to court get fined, but rarely punished, so they bankroll their way out and are back on the streets the next day. If we are lucky enough to get a firm conviction on, say, a drug dealer, the jail is so crowded that most of the time the court slaps them with an ankle bracelet and puts them on house arrest. Care to guess where they probably dealt drugs from in the first place? Home."

John took a second to let the words take hold before he continued. "Now, just think of this: that's just the drug dealers. We also have child molesters, rapists, habitual DUI offenders, and much, much more running around out there."

"But there's a sex offender registry in place for the perverts to keep them in check and you can revoke licenses for the DUI offenders. That helps keep them under control."

"Guess again. The sex offender registry is required, but there are a lot who choose not to register when they move, and they move a lot. I couldn't begin to tell you how many I've personally arrested that are driving revoked because of DUIs. You see, it's only the ones who have a conscience that are bothered by breaking the law. Those aren't the ones that cause the trouble typically. It's the ones that don't mind that you have to watch out for. If they want something bad enough and don't care if they

Reduction

break a law to get it, they will. If it works and they get to stay out of jail, they'll do it again."

"OK, so why not hire more officers to cover the trouble spots and catch these guys in the act? Isn't that what the politicians always talk about?"

"Adding more officers would be a great idea except for two things. First, there's not enough extra money in the budget to hire that many extra officers. Second, in order to have enough officers to really be effective, half the population would have to be in uniform in order to watch the other half that isn't. Then who would pay their salaries?

"Something most people don't understand is that law enforcement is not a prevention of crime. Most of the time we aren't catching people in the act of committing a crime, we're filling out reports about one that's already happened. We can't arrest anyone for a crime that hasn't happened yet. We just have to clean up the mess that's left behind so they can't do it again. Someone has to be a victim before we can even begin to do our jobs in most cases. There are exceptions, but for most crimes that's the way it works. Like it or not."

Mark had never thought about it in those terms before, but it made sense. You rarely ever heard of an officer walking up on a robbery or rape in progress, but you always heard about an investigation and search for suspects afterward.

"So, if there isn't enough money to hire more officers, how would I get paid?"

"The Chief has an idea of how to manage that. I'm guessing that it will actually come from several different sources, but it would be compiled into a cash payment to you so there's no tracing it back. Small movements of money from different places in the budget won't be missed and can easily be accounted for. He's got a plan and I don't want to know the details, just like he doesn't want to know about who you are or how you will do the jobs given to you. If he has no idea, he can't be connected. All communication and assignments would be handled through me directly, and on disposable cell phones or drops. Discretion would be crucial. Nobody, and I mean nobody, can know about this. Not even Angie. Like they say on the movies, this conversation didn't even happen."

"Like 007, huh?"

"More like the Punisher or Batman I'd think."

"Nah, both of them lost their families. I just lost my job. So, what should I tell Angie that I'm doing? I mean, she's going to ask."

"Tell her you're going hunting. Tell her you have some errands to run. Most of your work would likely take place at night when she's asleep, so you could tell her you are helping out for the night shift with janitorial work or something."

"What about as a night shift dispatcher?"

Reduction

"No good. That puts you too close to the telephone, and you might not want to have a phone ring when you're on a job. It should be something that you can't be distracted easily doing, but try to make it something that won't make her worry too much. You don't need that extra stress at home."

"One more question," Mark studied the offer momentarily, "Why do you think I would be good at something like this? Don't you have guys already on the force that could do this?"

"We have guys with the skills in the SWAT team to pull it off, but they are already stretched thin as it is. Anything more would be dangerous. Most of our patrolmen don't have much experience with a firearm beyond what they get at the academy and at annual qualification, so that takes them out of the equation. Besides, if it was a formal police action there would be hell to pay from the public outcry and law suits that would follow. Besides that the paperwork for an arrest is already a nuisance, can you imagine the nightmare that goes along with an officer involved shooting? People get fired for that even when it's done in self defense and the paper work is right!

"You're a natural when it comes to shooting. I'd say you're as good if not better than any sniper on the force, plus you know how to get in close if you have to. You're a thinker, too. You don't just run out and pop a target, you think the process through before you take your shot. That makes you careful. That means you are less likely to leave a trace. Now, here's where it gets tricky.

"Since you aren't 'officially' an officer, and since you would be actually shooting people, you will be viewed as a vigilante. The department will treat any news of you that way and the Chief will have people looking for you. Now, he won't put a lot of people on the job, but to satisfy the public he has to make it look like we're investigating the situation. Since I am the only one who knows you and the Chief will disavow any knowledge of your activity, you have to be *extremely* careful. Every other officer, no matter what they think of what you are doing, is charged with the responsibility of arresting people, anyone, who break the law. In this case, that would include you."

"So, let me see if I understand this. You are asking me to go out on behalf of the department and kill bad guys to save money, lawsuits, and paperwork but every time I drop someone there's a chance I could be arrested for it. I can't tell anyone what I'm doing and the Chief, even though he knows about it, will lie and say he doesn't. Does that pretty well sum it up?"

John smiled, "Yep, that's the gist. Any other questions?"

"Oh, yeah. Tons."

Reduction

Mark studied the offer some more, still not quite believing what had been presented to him. After a few minutes he had to ask, "Where do I get the weapons?"

"Well, I'd say you've already got them. I would suggest buying some different things, though. Maybe an SKS or AK, something the gang-bangers would likely have. That would make it easier to sell as turf violence. Maybe invest in a different long range rifle so that the rifling couldn't be tracked back to yours. I would also consider a suppressor, I can help you get the approval for one. Of course, that's an NFA item and would take longer to get, plus it would have a paper trail, so you wouldn't want to use it much."

"Could I use it as a pattern and make one? You know, one that couldn't be traced?"

"That would be a direct violation of the National Firearms Act. You're talking about a felony."

"As opposed to murder? Where exactly is the line drawn? I mean I'm no legal expert, but isn't this whole meeting technically committing conspiracy?"

John hadn't considered that before, but Mark was right. Just by having the conversation he was breaking the law and could jeopardize not only his job, but that of the Chief as well. Finally he said, "Well, I'll leave that up to you. Just don't tell me anything about it. Ignorance is bliss."

"Well, I know of at least three really ignorant people then," Mark popped back, "Ok, so, how much does this pay?"

"Well, that kind of depends on you. Would you rather get paid by the job or by the month?"

"How do you mean?"

Reduction

"OK, do you know how much it costs the taxpayers to keep someone behind bars?"

Mark shook his head. He hadn't really given it much thought.

"Depending on what level of incarceration you look at, local lock-up, state pen, etc., the average is between $40,000 and $60,000 per year, per prisoner."

Mark's eyes bulged at the figure and his jaw dropped slightly.

"That's more than most people made at the plant!"

"Yeah, tell me about it. That's more than most folks get paid to arrest them and keep them in there. Anyway, add to that figure the cost to actually carry the case to court, and the cost to pay for the resources you had to have for the initial arrest, plus the appeals that will inevitably follow, and don't forget the time and money for an investigation and rounding up witnesses. The list goes on and on. A simple arrest starts to get expensive really fast. If the guy is convicted then the cost to the taxpayer skyrockets. All because someone doesn't want to play by the rules.

"The way we looked at it was that you'd be saving the taxpayers at least the forty thousand a year, so that's our base target salary. What we had talked about was either setting up a kind of salary structure, where you would get a set amount each month for services rendered, or paying you by the job. Either way has its benefits and its drawbacks. A salary would be more complicated to set up, but it would pretty much guarantee you regular money each month. Payment by the job could be at your discretion and give you control of when you got paid. It could also mean that the jobs could be rated for difficulty. More difficult targets could pay more money and so on. It would be easier to hide the smaller amounts and could possibly get you more cash in hand. The choice would be yours. Either way, we expect to see about $40,000 or so annually. Like I said, it could be more or less, depending on how you want to work it."

"When do I need to let you know something?"

"Take your time and think it over. I know it's a lot to digest and you don't need to jump in without serious consideration. Just don't take too long, after all it will take some time to get the payment structure worked out, especially if you want a regular check."

"Okay," was all he could say. Was he actually going to consider doing this? What on earth would Angie say? Nothing. She could never know. Could he keep it a secret? Mark's mind raced with the complexity of it all. Just then his attention was drawn back to the range.

"You ready to run the AR's?"

"Yeah, sure. Looks like I might need the practice."

Chapter 2

Two weeks later Mark was in the workshop reading up on suppressors when his cell phone rang. It was John. Time to get to work. He had spent the past several days consuming every detail about how suppressors worked and how they didn't, examining prints where he could find them and studying ballistics for various calibers. Now he was ready to start prototyping, but he needed materials and a test platform. That cost money that he didn't have to spare, so the first job would be a loud one.

"What's up?"

"Not much man. You busy for lunch?"

"Nope. No cash to spare, so what do you want me to fix?"

"My treat. I don't have a lot of time. Court's in recess for a couple of hours, then I have to get

Reduction

back. Why don't you meet me at Victoria's in 20 minutes?"

"Victoria's? Man you eat high on the hog these days. Dahlgren paying you enough to feed both of us there?" Mark laughed.

"There's nothing wrong with splurging for a friend every now and then. What do you say?"

"What do you think? You know when the last time I had a steak was? If it didn't come onto the property with horns or scales I haven't eaten it in weeks," Mark laughed again, "I'll be there."

"See you in a few then."

Mark hung up and grabbed his sunglasses. He looked around the shop and decided it was sanitary enough that anyone who came in wouldn't realize what he had been doing. Not that it mattered because he was the only one home and would be until nearly 5:00 when Angie came in with the kids.

Reduction

He plopped into the driver's seat of the truck and headed down the driveway into town. While they didn't live far out in the country, it was nice to have a few acres around and gave him a peace of mind that he knew he would never get in the city.

The drive in was uneventful and he arrived with plenty of time to meet his friend in the foyer of the restaurant. Victoria's wasn't a terribly expensive place, but it was well known for the quality of food and the prices did reflect that. A popular place for business meetings during the day and romantic dinners at night, the business usually had a modest crowd whenever the doors were open. Today was no different. The nice thing about the place was that, even though it was so popular, there were plenty of places to carry on a casual, private conversation without worrying too much about being disturbed.

The hostess quickly got to the pair of them and ushered them through the dining room to a table in the back corner overlooking the rest of the room.

"Will this be OK?"

"Perfect, "Thompson replied, "You must have read my mind."

"We have enough policemen come in that we know you guys like your privacy," she smiled, "and a place to watch the door from. Your server will be with you in a minute. Is there anything you need until then?"

"No, thanks. I think we'll be alright."

The young lady turned sharply and headed back to the rostrum at the entrance where another group was already massing. Mark turned his attention back to the man across from him, curious about the large envelope that lay on the table by his left arm.

"Is that what I think it is?"

Reduction

"Nope. It's not your winning lottery ticket," Thompson smiled, "It's your first opportunity. You want to order first or get into the details now?"

Mark didn't have time to reply as the server stepped up to the table side.

"Hi, guys. My name's Amber and I'll be your server today. Do you need another minute or are you ready?"

"I know what I want, how 'bout you?"

Thompson scoured the menu once more and quickly said, "Yeah, I'm ready. Just give me the Cajun salad and a glass of water, please."

"And for you, sir?"

"I think I'll have the surf and turf with grilled shrimp and make my steak medium well, please. Oh, and give me a sweet tea for the drink. Thanks."

"Alright, guys, I'll get your order in and bring your drinks back in a minute."

"Thanks," both men replied almost in unison.

As she made her way back toward the kitchen John turned his attention back to the conversation at hand.

"I guess we'll order first," he smiled, "Now, where were we?"

"The envelope, please."

Thompson pushed the brown pouch across the table and watched Mark peel the flap open, peeking in to see the contents without actually removing anything.

"Chief thinks it would be best to start small and see if we can't establish a precedent, you know, knock out some of the underpinning so to speak and see who else falls. Maybe if folks see what getting in on the ground level can get you they won't care to get in at all."

"What's the pay for this one?"

"He's a small time pusher on the east side of town. You'll be seeing the area a lot, trust me. Since

Reduction

he's not high on the pole, we've got him priced out at $2500. Should be an easy target, he doesn't try to hide very much. Hell, the last 4 times he's been picked up he was under a carport set at the intersection of Cedar and 11th with a bunch of his 'associates' dealing in broad daylight. Don't get me wrong, he's got folks under him, runners and lookouts and the like. Most of them will be armed, but it'll be pistols and knives. Nothing heavy."

"Any extra for any of his pals?"

"Not this time around. Let's take him first and see what happens in their organization. Oh, one more thing. Chief doesn't care at all for anyone who is involved in a sexual assault case. Seems a few years ago he had a niece that was gang raped in Memphis. They never caught the guys. She never got over it. Killed herself a couple of years later. This little guy is a suspect in a similar case, but we've never been able to pin anything on him. We can't say that he was definitely involved, but we know some of his buddies were. They've been picked up, but nobody would talk about this one. Loyalty and all."

"Where can I find him?"

Thompson grabbed a napkin and quickly scratched out a map of the area, indicating with surprising detail possible vantage points and distances, fallback points and exit strategies. It became clear that John would pull the trigger himself if he could and he had put considerable forethought into the plan. It was a side of his friend he had never seen though he suspected it was probably there.

The remainder of the lunch meeting was filled with talk of guns and tactics, practical considerations before each job and techniques to scout an area without looking like he was scouting the area. John gave him some ideas for how to pick up extra firearms to work with that would be more difficult to trace back and were common to the gangs and punks around the areas he would work in.

As lunch drew to a close and they prepared to head their separate ways, Thompson reached into his jacket pocket and produced a small slip of paper and a plain pre-paid cell phone which he quietly handed off to Himes. He slowly opened it and smiled.

"What's this? A call sign?"

"Something like that. We figured there may be times that you might need to be in radio contact or may not feel comfortable using names over the phone, even though you'll be using a throw-away, so there you go. From now on you'll be known as Specter. The ghost-like, long arm of the law."

"One more question. How do I let you know if the job has been done? Do you want me to call or what?"

"Nope. We'll know when the dispatcher starts getting calls. If you feel that you need to advise us otherwise, just call my throw away and leave a simple message. No need for details. The number's already in your address book. Oh, and if you need to replace the phone be sure and destroy it. Wipe it down for prints and scatter the parts across several trash cans if you have to, but don't leave any way for it to be tracked."

"Does anyone else have this number?"

"Probably, it's a disposable, after all. Just don't answer it unless it's me. You'll know if it is. I have the same issue on my end to deal with."

Mark thought for a moment. He almost hated to ask, but felt like he needed to know the parameters in which he had to work.

"Got a time frame?"

"A deadline?" Thompson smiled at his own macabre joke, "Nope. No rush. Just keep it clean and quiet. Any questions, give me a call." He glanced at his watch, "I need to be going so I can see how many of my cases get to walk."

Reduction

"Alright then. Have fun." Mark smiled at his own ironic joke.

"You too. And, Mark,"

"Yeah?"

"Be careful out there."

"Can't afford not to."

Thompson headed toward the door with the ticket in hand as Mark picked up his packet and phone and followed suit. Soon he was back in the comfort of his workshop, papers scattered over the large build table in the center and a cup of hot coffee toward the edge. Mug shots and fingerprint cards, arrest records and evidence photos, a whole history of the 28-year-old male littered his work space. All copies for him to pour over and then destroy afterward. No traces.

The arrest record was impressive. He had been a busy man for a number of years, and managed to walk away from most of it with slaps on the wrist.

Reduction

One conviction for intent to sell resulted in a six month stay in the county jail and parole following which he quickly broke. The original sentence was for 11 months and 29 days, but due to overcrowding he had been cut loose early. Not long after he was back to finish it out.

Himes studied the man's files until time for the family to come home, then stuffed them back into the envelope and tucked it away among the many manuals and technical books that filled his bookshelf. Now he just had to figure out what to tell Angie.

He made his way to the house and slipped in the back door, kicking his shoes off just inside and heading to the kitchen to see what they had to pick from for dinner. They still had some venison and some bacon and eggs, thanks to a neighbor down the road. The man had needed a repair part made for an old tractor and Mark had been happy to help out so they had bartered a pound of bacon and some farm fresh eggs for the exchange. That was good enough for him, and he knew the kids would love breakfast for dinner for a change. With that he began digging out baking sheets and bowls for the feast.

Mark wasn't a bad cook, he just didn't care to very often. With all the free time he'd had since losing his job he had taken on the responsibility of cooking and cleaning more often as a way to manage Angie's stress as much as his own and, he had to admit, he was getting good at it.

The front door swung open and two pairs of thundering feet could be heard bursting through the hallway. As the storm door closed Angie let her own presence be known.

"Hi, honey! We're home!"

"I never would have guessed. Did you have a good day?"

"Just another day in paradise. How was yours? Any call backs today?"

"No. I may have a little something to do for John in the next couple of weeks, but I'm not sure when."

"Oh, really? What's John got going on?"

"Hmm? Nothing much. He just mentioned that he might need some help with a varmint problem he's been dealing with." It wasn't so much a lie as a distortion of facts. That made the bad taste in his mouth a bit more palpable.

"Varmint trouble? He doesn't have enough land to have varmint trouble. I mean, he practically lives in town. It's not like he has coyotes running through the yard every night, or deer getting into his garden when he's asleep."

"Um, yeah, well, it may not be for him. It could be for someone else, but he wanted me to take care of it since I needed something to do. I'll find out more later."

Reduction

"Whatever. Just be sure you get paid for it. We need every dime we can get right now. Mmm," she said as she peered over his shoulder, "what's cooking, good looking?"

"I thought we might have breakfast tonight for a change and see what the Roberts' have in the way of bacon. Did you know they cure their own pork bellies and make their own bacon?"

"I knew they had a few hogs, but I never thought to ask what they did with them."

"You know, we have a few acres more than they do," Mark began.

Angie shut him down in mid-thought, "And they know what they're doing with animals too. The last thing we need is a bunch of pigs running around making a mess. You and all of your machine shop oils and grit are more than enough for me." She smiled at her husband and let a little laugh slip.

Reduction

"Fair enough," he said, "I wouldn't know what to do with a hog anyway. Speaking of which, can you check the bacon for me? It should be close to done. As soon as I can have the oven I have biscuits waiting on the sidelines."

"Scratch biscuits? You are the man, babe."

"Oh sure, you say that now. Just wait until you taste it, then you'll change your tune." He laughed. At least both of them were still able to joke and pick playfully. He had heard through the grapevine that some of his co-workers were having considerable marital trouble following the layoffs.

The next morning, after everyone else had gone for the day, Mark got into his truck and drove into town, then across the river to the east side. He found a parking garage within site of the area he needed to see that John had suggested for a surveillance point and drove to the top level where he parked facing the 11th Avenue intersection.

Reduction

There, looking almost directly down Cedar he could make out the shape of a small metal carport resting just off the edge of the pavement. Under the shade of the corrugated metal roof he could make out a number of shadowy figures, but from this distance he couldn't be sure of how many were there. He reached over behind the passenger side seat and produced his spotting scope and aimed it toward the simple structure. There, strutting about like a celebrity with his own entourage, was his target.

The distance measured almost 600 yards from where he sat. That would be a complicated shot, but within the range of his '06. It was a bit too open up on top, but maybe a lower level could work. John had also mentioned an old apartment building nearby, just a few stories tall and abandoned. That might be a good alternate if the line of sight was good enough. It could be tricky checking it out in the daytime. Then again it could be tricky at night as well.

Reduction

After scanning the area with the spotting scope he located the building and studied it for a while. Sure enough it looked to be abandoned, and by his range finder it was almost 150 yards closer. That meant a slight adjustment from his present scope setting, but not too bad. Windage could be a problem as the streets would play havoc with wind direction and velocity, so it would be best to watch for a calm forecast.

After a lengthy observation of both target and surrounding, Himes decided to cast his worries aside and check the building out. Rather than drive his truck over he decided it was best to strap on his .45 and walk. It would take longer, but he could also see the general layout of the surrounding neighborhood and the people he would be disturbing when he took his shot.

His stroll taught him a number of things very quickly. For one thing, a clean shaven Caucasian was certainly an oddity in this area. For another, most people in the area didn't really care who walked by them on the street, they rarely lifted their eyes to see anyway. Himes thought for a minute that a gunshot in this part of town probably wouldn't even wake most people, let alone merit a call to the police. He made a mental note to let Thompson know when the job was done, otherwise he feared the body would rot in the street.

He reached the building and casually stopped to tie his shoe and glance around. The fence around it was in poor shape in the best of places and the door looked to have been busted down some years earlier. Litter on the lawn made him cautious about walking there, so he tried to spot a cleaner, quieter access that had a smaller chance of being strewn with needles and broken crack pipes. Then he spotted a small trail leading across the back yard. It looked like some kind of animal trail and he wondered if there could be anything rabid calling the place home. He eased his way around to the rear and stole into the structure as quietly as possible, making sure no prying eyes were on him. The stairway was as close to a death trap as he had ever seen, but seemed sturdy enough to carry his weight.

"I wonder how many termites are actually holding this thing together," He thought to himself. He made his way to the uppermost floor and began carefully looking out the windows for the best vantage point. As he stepped into the third room he noticed that the window to his right perfectly framed the intersection with a clear shot at the entire structure. A photographer couldn't have posed the shot better. The only problem was going to be getting out.

Getting down the five flights of steps was dangerous enough without being in a hurry. Trying to navigate the steps with a rifle and in a hurry could be

Reduction

a very hazardous issue indeed. The prospect of shooting from the parking garage was looking better.

Himes made his way back down and stealthily out, then down a side street and circled back to the garage taking care not to use the same route out that he did in to the building. As he sat on the upper level of the garage once again he took one more look through the scope. That's when he realized that, to further complicate things, it would have to be a daytime shot. It was time to detail the plan.

A few days later he headed back to the garage for the last time. The wind was calm, with an average five mile per hour breeze from time to time. Clouds threatened rain at any time and, as a matter of fact, a light drizzle had already begun to fall. Himes was concerned that the weather might make his target decide to stay home. He backed his truck in the garage parking space with the tailgate facing the direction of the carport and slipped out of the cab and into the bed. As a precaution he had pulled his old tonneau bed cover out of storage and snapped it on a couple of days earlier.

To his luck the garage was pretty empty on the upper levels and with the weather the top level was completely unoccupied. He set up a sandbag for a makeshift rest and tried to get his breathing regulated. Looking through the scope he saw that the lure of easy money was stronger than the urge to stay warm and dry. His objective was there, just like before, but with only a few of his acquaintances this time. He took a few minutes to clear his mind and ready himself for the shot, then snuggled up to the rifle and tucked the stock into his shoulder. He steadied himself and peered through the scope.

Down the street, he could clearly see the carport. In front of it a pair of tail lights glowed brightly. His man rushed to the driver's side window and quickly completed the transaction, and returned to the shelter to talk with his friends. Himes had an idea.

A few minutes later another vehicle pulled up and stopped in front of the would be apothecary. Before the vehicle came to a stop his man was already approaching the window, hands in his pockets and ready to deal. With the overcast sky this was going to be a loud one. No chance for a follow up.

Deep breath.

He reached the window.

Let some out.

He took the money.

Press the trigger, don't yank.

As the hand came out of the pocket the rifle cracked. Himes saw the body twitch as a spray of crimson appeared where the head was only a fraction of a second before. He pulled back the magnification to make sure the target was down and confirm the kill. He could see the others jump and stare as the shock of what had happened began to take hold. One of the men suddenly made the connection that the driver must have been the gunman and swung his pistol toward the door of the vehicle.

Himes considered taking the man down, but knew that a second shot would give his location away and, if they took the time to pay attention, they would see that the driver probably didn't have a weapon. The cold truth of it was that it wasn't his problem. The target lay sprawled across the edge of the pavement, a pool of blood where part of the head should have been. Reduced to a pile, he thought. Reduced.

He shoved the rifle aside and crawled out of the bed. As he closed the tailgate he heard a muffled "pop, pop, pop" from the direction of the intersection mingled with the distinct sound of tires squealing. Looking back he saw the buyer speeding away as the thugs stormed out into the street, pistols blazing. Himes stood for a moment and realized that he needed to be on the move himself. With all that gunfire someone would tell the police and he didn't need anyone searching his vehicle right now.

Once he was safely away, he pulled over and flipped out his phone. He began a new text message with the simple message "Reduction complete" and sent it off to Thompson.

A few hours later, while studying the contents of the cupboard again, Himes' home phone rang. The caller I.D. indicated that it was Thompson's cell phone. Mark picked it up and strode back to the kitchen.

"How's it going?"

"Not bad. Yourself?"

"Well, so far so good. Not sure what we're doing for dinner tonight yet, but other than that not bad. What's up?"

Reduction

"I thought I might drop you a line and see what you had going on this afternoon. I have a little present for you. Wanted to drop it by."

"A present? For me? Aww, you shouldn't have." To listen to his voice you would never suspect that Mark had just killed a man that morning, "Sure. What time are you wanting to come by?"

"I'll be tied up until around 3:30 or 4:00. Will that be too late?"

"Nah, Angie won't be home until around 5:00. Oh, if you can't get an answer at the door come around to the shop. I may be in there."

"Sure thing. I'll see you in a couple of hours."

"Sounds good. See you then." Mark clicked the phone off and laid it on the counter, returning to his search for dinner ingredients.

Around 4:30 Thompson pulled up to the house and walked up to the front door. He rang the doorbell with no response so he tried knocking. After all, sometimes transformers wore out or chimes got stuck. Still no answer. Then he remembered that Himes could be in his metal shop around back so that's where he headed.

As he stepped up to the door he could hear machinery running and knew that Himes was inside. He knocked on the door then poked his head in to announce his arrival.

"Hey, man. I'm here!" He called across the room. Mark stood in front of a lathe working on what looked like some sort of aluminum can. He turned slightly then motioned John in.

Thompson spied a chair near the workbench and a small refrigerator in the corner. Making himself at home he slipped over to the refrigerator and grabbed a soft drink, then made himself comfortable in the chair. Drawings littered the workbench of oddly shaped cylindrical design. Almost like cones fused to cylinders with small holes here and there.

Reduction

Thompson wondered what the components were then assumed that Himes had picked up some sort of side project for an extra dollar. Perhaps some sort of engine component? They did look slightly like some sort of piston. As he sat filled with curiosity he heard the lathe wind down. Mark removed one of the odd piston looking pieces from the machine and headed toward the table.

"What are you working on?" Thompson asked with a curious grin.

"Oh," Himes began, "Just a little side project." He dropped the small metal piece on the table and pulled a stool over. "What's up?

"Nothing much. I just thought you might want this." Thompson produced a small security envelope and handed it over to Himes.

He smiled a sheepish grin as he opened the envelope, spying $2500 in small bills within, then tucked it away in his pocket.

"Nice doing business with you." He said, still sporting his grin.

"Well, speaking of business," Thompson said, "How is that bit of business sitting with you? You felling OK?"

"Fine. I actually haven't thought about it much to be honest. I've been keeping busy, you know."

"Oh, OK. I don't want you to go all PTSD on me or anything. If you start having trouble dealing with this you let me know, alright?"

"Sure," Himes said, a trace of his grin still on his face, "but really, I'm fine. If I start having nightmares or wetting the bed you'll be the first one I'll call." A broad grin spread across his face and he turned to fiddle with the component he'd just made.

"I'm serious, Mark. I've seen some tough guys that couldn't do my job, let alone what we've asked you to do. If you need counseling you let me know."

Reduction

He paused momentarily, then decided to push the topic just a bit further, "*How* are you dealing with it? What are you doing?"

Himes sat silently for a second before he responded, avoiding eye contact at first and shrugging his shoulders in an almost child-like fashion.

"You'll probably think it's stupid," he smiled.

"Come on. Spit it out."

"Well, when I hunt deer, for example, I'm taking a life to keep my family alive. That deer has never done a thing to me." He paused again, "But if my family's going to eat, I have to put food on the table. It's a simple matter of priority. That deer's life is not as important to me as my family's."

John sat at the table studying Mark's expressions intently. He seemed pretty stable and calm. Whatever his method was it appeared to be working.

Reduction

"So, when I looked through the scope and saw the guy on the street, I just prioritized things in my mind. He'd never done anything to me, but he might have done something to someone else. His business was making people depend on drugs that could kill them. He was most likely a rapist. He had a history of theft and assault, which meant that rather than earn a living, he chose to take someone else's from them. He'd never done anything to me, but what if that was my son that he was dealing drugs to? What if it was my daughter that had been raped? What if it had been me that he had robbed or my wife he had assaulted? It became a priority to never give him the opportunity and to send a message to his friends that they need to change their line of work before they wound up like him."

Thompson sat silently for a minute. It was simple, but it seemed to work.

"OK, then," he said finally, "So, are you up for another assignment?"

"Let me get supper ready for the crew and then I'll get right on it."

"You don't have to jump on it right now," Thompson laughed, "but when you have a minute I'll leave this with you." He produced another brown envelope and laid it on the table.

"Have you disposed of the other information yet?"

"Yep. I ran it through our document shredder and then burnt it before I took the shot. I have a burn barrel out back for trash and the like, so I figured that was as good as any other method."

"Good. Is there anything you want to discuss about the job? Questions or concerns you might have?"

"Well, the distance was a concern, but not a problem. I figured the noise would be a problem, but his buddies apparently never heard it. They turned their pistols on the car that he was dealing with. Any word on what happened there?"

"Minor injuries reported, mostly from broken glass. The driver and passenger wouldn't say where they were when it happened or who was involved, so we can't pursue a case against the shooters. They're afraid we'll bust them for making a buy or being an accessory to murder or something. In any case it's nothing for you to worry about."

Himes looked relieved to know that no one else had been killed, but it showed once again how the system had its limitations. After a few minutes John stood up and looked at his watch. It was time for Angie and the kids to be home and he thought it best to leave.

"Tell you what, I'm going to get out of here. If you have any questions, give me a call. Otherwise, I guess I'll look for your message. Oh," he looked at his

Reduction

friend quizzically, "reduction? Where'd that come from?"

Mark smiled, "Well, it's like a reduction in manpower for the bad guys, so I thought it was a good way of phrasing it. You like?"

John laughed, "Yeah, that's pretty good. I'll talk to you later, man. Be careful."

As Thompson drove down the driveway Himes opened the brown envelope and removed the contents. Mug shots showed another young man, this one a bit older than the first, but still younger than himself. Another lengthy criminal history capped off with a pair of home invasions back to back. The first was essentially a burglary, but the second was particularly violent. No one had died, but there was an elderly homeowner that was seriously injured when he tried to resist. Witnesses had identified the man as he left the home.

Reduction

According to the information he could most probably be found at his girlfriend's apartment. Again Thompson had included a map of the area with key locations indicated. Himes couldn't help but notice that the parking garage he had used was only a mile or so from the address listed. That was out of the question. Two shots from the same platform would be setting a pattern. That was a good way to get yourself caught...or killed. There had to be another place.

Himes noticed that there was a circle around a large building that turned out to be an old manufacturing plant that had closed a few years earlier. It had potential, but there was the problem of proximity again. Closer to the apartment than his last shot, it was still looking like a four hundred yard shot or more. The problem was that with the orientation of the building there was no clear line of sight that he could see on the map. That meant recon. He would check it out later. Right now there was other work to do. Work that would be necessary for the success of future jobs.

He gathered the numerous pieces of machined aluminum and placed them on the table. Then he collected a small cylinder from a nearby cabinet and some other smaller threaded rings and components from a box on a different shelf. Moving back to the table he began to assemble the individual pieces into the suppressor he had been prototyping for the past few days. Tomorrow he would test fire it.

The next morning he grabbed the AR-15 and his prototype can and slipped out behind his workshop. Setting cans up at various distances up the gentle hillside that rose from the back yard he would walk his way up the field of fire noting accuracy and performance. If he had built it right he should see at least a 30 decibel reduction in muzzle noise. He returned to the shop to remove the muzzle brake from the rifle and slip the suppressor on. Loading one round in the magazine he took careful aim at the closest target.

"Man, I wish I had another way to do this," Himes thought as he settled behind the rear sight and acquired his sight picture.

With his hearing protection on he could hear nothing above the clack of the hammer striking the firing pin. The can flipped away from its position and Himes decided to load another round and try it without the muffs. With the next trigger pull he realized just how quiet the system was. Accuracy seemed to be a bit off, but the silencing effect was considerable. By the time Himes had moved out to the two hundred yard marker he knew he would have to do some modification to the unit. It was too long to be a quick rifle and it was shooting far to the left and low over the longer distances. Then again, he had never used this rifle for anything other than playing on the tactical range, so he had no idea what the long range capabilities really were.

He returned to the shop and began to re-examine the data that he had for the suppressor. He decided to make a couple of changes to the overall design to better suit his application before putting it to use. By the following week he would have a second prototype to test, especially since he had a little cash to invest in proper materials. He would deposit a good portion of what he had made into the bank account, of course, but discretion made him hesitant to deposit it all. He would need liquid cash for expenses relative to his new "job" such as fuel and ammo.

The following week he stepped out back and verified his zero without the suppressor attached and, with optics, could hit well past three hundred yards repeatedly. The rifle was zeroed and sound. Time for the new prototype. He reached over into the range

Reduction

box and produced the long, slim redesign and began to screw it onto the muzzle. This model slipped over the barrel almost to the front sight post and extended past the muzzle only about four inches. The hope was that the internal baffle modifications would redirect the majority of muzzle blast rearward to dissipate around the barrel. Shortly after the bullet left the barrel the expanding gasses would be diverted backwards and filter through the baffles, exhausting themselves before venting out.

Himes loaded a single round into the chamber and placed the rifle on a sandbag rest, sighting in the first target at fifty yards. He slipped on his ear and eye protection and raised the rifle to his cheek. He pressed the trigger and sent the round downrange with only a flutter of sound emanating from the rifle. He loaded a second round and slipped off his safety gear, then took aim at the 75 yard target. As he pressed the trigger a second time the .223 coughed shyly and the can flipped high in the air.

Repeating the process over and over again until he reached 225 yards, the maximum he could safely shoot on his property, the design proved sound and Himes smiled at his own success. It was time to move on to the next step in the process. He had to find an upper receiver to use with the suppressor that was good for long range shots but inexpensive enough that he could toss it if he had to. He loaded everything back into the range box and tucked it away in the shop where no one would think to look, then headed into the house to surf the internet.

Mark decided on a twenty inch heavy barreled upper receiver assembly. He found one at a local gun shop and managed to strike a reasonable deal to include the bolt carrier group as well. It was higher than ordering online, but there was no credit card trail to trace it back since he paid cash. The upper was

Reduction

built with a full length rail that would make mounting a scope easy and quick. While it wasn't the most expensive, free floated upper available and it probably couldn't drive tacks at five hundred yards, he didn't need it to. It was what it was: a tool to do a job.

He carried it back home and loaded up his range bag and some targets, then headed to his makeshift range. He wanted to check accuracy over distance before applying the suppressor. He placed a silhouette target out at 100 yards and another at the maximum 225 yards. Through the spotting scope he could easily make out the upper torsos and heads of each target. He focused on the 100 yard target first and zeroed his scope at center of mass. Satisfied with the grouping he moved to the head. He applied the suppressor and settled back behind the scope. The head shots landed exactly where he needed them to and he moved to the longest target. A few minutes later both targets sported three small .22 caliber holes, each touching the other, in the center of the A zone. The can had worked beyond Marks' expectations and the accuracy was dead on. It was almost time to go to work.

Mark headed out to the neighborhood and drove past the old manufacturing plant, taking care to look it over. Most of the windows and doors were broken or missing entirely. There was a large chain link fence surrounding the property, but areas of it had been compromised through the unchecked growth of small trees and vagrants. He found a safe location to park the truck and walked toward the aging structure. Today he was more conscious of his appearance than before. He wore some older clothes that were more worn and an old ball cap that was frayed along the bill and discolored. Hopefully his clothes and unshaven appearance would allow him to blend in better. He didn't want anyone to give him a second look.

Reduction

He reached the building and began to scan the fence for a possible opening and any signs of surveillance cameras. None of the meter bases showed available power to the structure, which meant that there shouldn't be any operating security cameras or alarms, despite the signs to the contrary placed at regular intervals along the fence. He spied a gap in the fence behind a thick growth of vegetation on an opposite corner and slowly made his way toward it. When he reached the opening he glanced around and tossed his small backpack through. He had seen no sign of movement inside the fence since he had been there and hoped that it would stay that way.

Mark made his way across the compound and into the lower floor of a massive assembly area. The room still contained traces of it's past. Everywhere he looked there were pipes and conduits, large breaker panels and switch boxes, and the footprints of assembly lines and large equipment could be seen everywhere. To his left he spotted a set of steel steps leading to the upper levels and he quietly made his way to them. He smiled to himself at the thought of the steel staircase as compared to the rickety wooden death trap at the old apartment house.

From the second level he moved upward yet again and eventually found a roof access hatch. He slowly opened the hatch and peeked around. There were a number of suitable positions he could shoot from and he was tempted to climb up and check each one. Then he realized that it would look awkward to see someone on the roof of an abandoned building in broad daylight with a spotting scope. It would be best to wait until dark to climb out. For now he would spot his target from an upper level window and get his range and angles.

He found a window looking down the street he needed and set up his spotting scope. Himes then pulled the map from the information packet out and identified the correct house. The range finder indicated a distance of roughly 325 yards. That would work well with the new upper.

He watched the house for a short while and scanned the neighborhood for any signs that his man might be around. After a short while he noticed the front door open and a young woman step onto the porch. She reached over into the mailbox mounted on the wall and removed the mail. He noticed that as she made her way to the front door she seemed to be speaking to someone. Could his target be inside? He needed his rifle just in case and he didn't bring it with him. He quickly decided to collect his equipment and come back later that evening.

As he stole his way down the stairway and out to the doorway his mind raced with the variables, not the least of which was the timing of the shot. If he had to make it at night there was no way to positively identify his target. Night vision equipment was not something he kept in his gun safe and certainly not something he could afford.

He started across the cracked and faded asphalt that once served as a shipping and receiving area and eased along the fence to the opening again. After tossing his bag through he stepped out and back onto the edge of the street. Turning to walk back to his truck he became aware of a car quietly approaching from behind. He stepped off the pavement as the vehicle slowed to a stop beside him. Himes turned his head when he heard the window roll down only to see the face of John Thompson looking back at him.

"I thought that was you," he said, "What brings you into these parts?"

"House hunting," Himes replied wryly, "This one has plenty of space and a lot of land, but it needs some work."

Reduction

Thompson laughed and glanced around, noticing that the reunion was getting unwanted attention. He placed the car in Park and stepped out, approaching his friend cautiously. As he came around the car he called to Himes, "Show me some I.D., buddy."

Himes looked confused by the sudden request and slowly fumbled for his wallet. Thompson came closer so that Himes could hear him, but his voice wouldn't carry far.

"Play along. We've got an audience behind the curtains and on the porches."

Thompson examined Himes' identification and acted as if he was calling it in. A few minutes later he told his friend to place his hands behind his back and then had him crawl in the back seat of the unmarked car. Thompson then got back into the driver's seat and the pair drove away from the old factory.

Reduction

"Where's your truck?"

"Parking lot a few blocks over. I thought it best to walk in."

"Good idea. How's the planning going?"

"So far, so good. One thing worries me, though. Oh, hang a right here."

"What's got you stumped?"

"I think he may be at the girlfriend's house right now. I can't be sure because I didn't actually *see* him."

"What? Right now? Why do you think that?"

"She came out and checked the mail and was talking to someone inside as she went back to the door. Does she have a roommate or kids?"

Thompson studied for a moment, then said, "Not that I'm aware of. I'm sure there aren't any kids, and I'm almost positive there's no roommate. I can double check to be sure."

Reduction

"Don't worry about it. I'm not pulling the trigger unless I have him in my sights, no one else. That's not what has me addled , though. It occurred to me that if he doesn't stick his head out until after dark I might not get the shot. I'm not equipped for night shooting."

"Hmm. I see your problem. I'll tell you what, let me do some digging and I'll see if I can help you out somehow."

Himes directed him to the parking lot and the pair pulled around to a secluded area where Thompson removed the cuffs. Mark thanked him and then headed back around to where the truck was parked. Soon he was on the way home, but he'd be back in a couple of hours.

Chapter 3

Mark laid prone on the old factory roof patiently waiting for the opportunity to eliminate his target. The sun would be down in a little while and his chance to take the man out would be practically gone. During the past three hours he had seen no movement at all from the house. He couldn't know if the man was still inside or not, but his gut told him he was. The man could have slipped out the back door without being seen, but Himes felt that he was still laying low inside.

From somewhere inside the old building Mark heard a faint thumping sound. It could have been footsteps, but they were faint and from his lofty position he couldn't be sure what level or direction the sound came from. He cautiously reached for his .45 that was tucked in his Milt Sparks Executive

Reduction

Companion and drew it from the holster. If the roof hatch opened he would at least have it handy. If anyone decided to camp out inside the building it would make egress a complicated issue, but the possibility was there. He hadn't noticed any signs of occupation during his recce of the facility, but he didn't look everywhere either. There could easily be several homeless people using the building for shelter below him. There was a separate access stairway toward the other end of the building, but he hadn't used it and wasn't sure of its condition.

Himes heard the rattle of the stairs behind him that lead to the roof. Someone was on the way up. His hand gripped the .45 and he turned his torso to acquire the door if he should have to use the weapon. A moment later the door swung open slowly and he could make out the shape of a man scanning the roof.

"Mark!" Came the whispered call across the roof. "Don't freak out, man. It's me, Thompson."

"What the hell are you doing up here?" Himes asked as his friend crept low to his position.

"What the hell is *that*?" Thompson asked as he motioned to the suppressed AR-15.

"Nothing you need to worry about," came the reply with a smirk, "Your turn."

"I told you I was going to try and help out, so let me show you what I came up with."

Thompson opened the small black case that he had brought with him. Inside was a black scope and covers. Thompson removed it and held it for Himes to see.

"Night vision. Generation 4. Never been used. We got these as part of a Homeland Security upgrade a few years ago and nobody has ever used them. I figured it might come in handy this evening."

Reduction

"That thing have good enough resolution to I.D. the guy from here? I thought they were kind of grainy and limited."

"Man, with this I can count the freckles on a gnat's ass at 200 yards," Thompson joked, "It'll be enough."

"I hope you're right," Himes replied, "Night's coming on fast and my visibility will be nothing here in a little while. Fire that thing up and let's see how many freckles are buzzing about."

"What about your toy?" Thompson asked, "That thing effective at all?

"It's quieter than a gnat's ass at 200 yards." Mark smiled to himself.

Thompson peered through the optic down the street before them and scanned the address. Nothing moved. He panned into the back yard, which was partly obscured by trees, but couldn't see any movement there either. The pair sat in silence for over two hours before activity caught their attention.

The back door opened and the pair immediately turned their eyes toward the light spilling across the darkening lawn. Between the branches of the sparse trees and scrubby, unkempt hedges that lined the perimeter of the back yard they could make out a silhouette. There wasn't a clear enough vantage to determine if it was male or female, so he kept watching, hoping there would be an opportunity for identification.

After a few minutes the figure returned to the back door, this time illuminated in the glow of the small porch light. Male. It could be the target, but the moment had passed before an adequate I.D. could be made. It would be nearly an hour before the house would capture their attention again.

The front sidewalk brightened as the front door swung open. A pair of figures stood momentarily in the opening and talked. Through the night vision scope Thompson could clearly see that it was a man and a woman, but the man's back was turned to them, so he couldn't positively identify him.

"Are you seeing them?" Thompson whispered, never taking his eyes from the optic.

"Got 'em," came the reply from Himes, "Is that our man?"

"Wait for it. I'll let *you* know as soon as *I* do."

The next few minutes passed like an eternity as the pair watched and waited. Finally, the conversation between the mysterious duo came to an end and the man leaned in to kiss the woman. When he turned Thompson could make out the man's face clearly. There was no doubt this was the target.

"Take him out."

"Are you sure?"

"No doubt. If you get the shot, drop him."

Reduction

Mark zoomed his scope to maximum and tracked the target as he started down the front walk toward the curb. Just as he reached the edge of the yard he paused, as if he had forgotten something. He turned and faced the house again, taking a half-step toward the building and calling back to the woman. At that distance the conversation couldn't be heard, but it didn't matter. As he turned his attention back toward the street Himes tightened his grip on the trigger.

Mark took a breath and exhaled slightly, focusing on the crosshairs resting squarely on the man's head some 300 yards away. As he pressed the trigger the AR coughed and the round was away. Through the scope he could see the figure suddenly jerk as the round found its mark, embedding deeply into the side of the man's skull. He staggered to the right, as if by sheer will he was determined to go about his business. Before he could move a full step the rifle coughed again and the second round plunged into the chest cavity under his left arm. He stopped cold and slumped to the ground, twitching as his nerves tried in desperation to cope with the sudden shock. A scream echoed through the darkened street as a shadowy figure raced to the silent body.

"Time to go." John said flatly.

"Quietly, if you don't mind." Mark commented, carefully breaking the rifle and suppressor down and tucking them into a duffel bag of pillows and dirty clothes he had brought to compliment his disguise. The pair descended the staircase and stole their way across the compound and onto the streets. They had successfully completed the primary objective of the night. Now they had to finish the job and make it home without being caught.

As they neared the parking lot Mark had used earlier they noticed an increased police presence in the nearby neighborhood. Through the houses and buildings an intermittent reflection of blue and red lights could be seen and the sirens of ambulances and police cars still echoed through the alley ways and streets as responders arrived on the scene.

"Go home, man," John said to his friend, "Good work. I'll talk to you tomorrow."

Mark stepped toward the truck and placed the duffel bag on the seat.

"Sounds good. Thanks for the assist. No way I could have done that without you."

Two vehicles came to life and headed in opposite directions through the city streets. It wouldn't take very long before Mark would be home and he was tired. He never realized how draining it could be to just lay around for hours, but when the stress of the task was added into the equation it became a chore indeed. He wanted to crawl into the bed and pass out, but there were things that had to be done first. He needed to make sure that the tools were properly cleaned and stored and that the suppressor was likewise wiped down and stored in its own special place. It would be another couple of hours before his head would see the pillow.

Mark got up early and fixed breakfast while Angie was still in the shower. Soon he would have to wake the kids and get them off to school, but for right then he enjoyed the peace and quiet of the morning. After a few minutes Angie strolled into the kitchen for her morning coffee and was surprised to see the cup already filled and waiting.

"Well, good morning, good looking," she announced.

"Good morning. How'd you sleep?"

"Pretty well. You?"

"Like a rock. What can I get you for breakfast this morning?" Mark turned his attention to the griddle where an assortment of homemade pancakes was almost ready to be flipped.

"Oh, I'll be more than happy to take some of those off your hands," she smiled, motioning to the pancakes, "Oh, have you watched the weather yet?"

"Nope. I was enjoying the silence. Hang on a second and I'll hook that up for you."

Mark eyed the griddle once more before stepping to a small television on the countertop that Angie liked to watch from time to time while cooking big meals. He tuned in one of the local stations just as the weather portion was coming to a close.

"Looks like we missed it. Oh, well, it'll be on again in a few minutes."

"Yeah," she said, "that's the good thing about morning news programs."

She took another sip of her coffee as the camera shifted to the news desk and the anchor began recapping the morning's top stories.

Reduction

"Investigators are still looking for information regarding the shooting death of an east side drug dealer while another man was gunned down just a few blocks away last night. Police Chief Mike Dahlgren announced yesterday that while they did not have a definite suspect in the slaying evidence strongly indicated that it was drug related.

"Only a few blocks away from the first shooting, police responded to another incident around 10:30 last night. Police have not released the name of the victim, but have said that they do have several people of interest that they want to talk to."

"I don't know what the world is coming to," Angie said as she took the first bite, "I mean, it seems like every time you hear the news someone is getting killed or raped. Sometimes I just wish we could move off to an island somewhere and start our own country."

Reduction

She took another bite as the anchor continued, "Neighbors say they heard no gunfire and reports from the scene say there is very little in the way of evidence. The victim reportedly lived with his girlfriend and was shot as he left to go to work."

As the anchor turned the broadcast over to the traffic and weather segments Mark studied Angie's face. Should he say something? Would she understand that he was trying to help the police and them by doing the job he'd been asked to do? The want to discuss it was overshadowed by the need to keep it quiet. Angie was no gossip but he feared that, in struggling to comprehend the manner of work, she might say something to someone who was. That would be disastrous for everyone involved. No, it was best to labor on and not say a word.

It wasn't long before she and the kids were away for the day and he sat alone again in the quiet of the house. He sipped at his own coffee in silence,

Reduction

considering his options for the day. There was always something to do in the shop. He'd start there.

As he sat at his workbench the events of the previous night kept playing over in his mind. It didn't bother him that he had taken a man's life. The unrelenting nuisance was that it took two shots to do it. He knew that the first shot was lethal. It had to be. The distance was well within the range of the caliber and the rifle had been shooting dead on. Still, the man had taken the hit and continued to walk. Apparently, Mark needed to consider a more powerful caliber for this type of work.

Having the semi-auto capability for quick follow up shots had made the difference, but greater stopping power would negate the need for a follow up at all. The .30-06 had more than enough power, but the bolt action slowed it down for multiple shots. Maybe he should invest in a .308, after all that was a common sniper round and there were plenty of semi-automatic versions out there. Mark wasn't one for the tactical, military style rifles, but if he could find something for a reasonable price that could hold accuracy well beyond 500 yards or so it was worth at least looking in to.

He decided that whatever he bought it would also need to be suppressed, but that meant building another suppressor and threading the barrel followed by the test firing that made him so very uncomfortable. Still, when the reporter announced that no shots had been heard it took a load of weight off his shoulders. He knew that it had been worth the effort to conceal his location. More research would be necessary to figure out how to soften the bark of such a large round.

Mark reached over into the bookshelf and slipped out the notebook of suppressor information he had been compiling over the past few weeks. Shuffling through the pages he found what he was

Reduction

looking for and began spreading the papers across the table. Soon the surface was awash with specs and photos, sketches and calculations for the design and construction of a .308 suppressor.

Himes poured over the data and lost track of time. Had it not been for the rumbling of his stomach he would have worked clean through lunch trying to devise an effective approach to fabrication. He put things on hold and moved to the house for a quick bite. While eating he decided to scour the internet for rifles to see what was available and a ballpark price.

It wasn't long before he came across an online classified listing for firearms. From there he was able to narrow down the criteria and found several items within a few miles of him that looked promising. There was a .308 caliber AR platform, a FN FAL in near new condition, an M1A SOCOM model, and a very nice Remington 700 tactical model that was factory threaded for a suppressor. Unfortunately it was a bolt action.

Reaching the third page of items in the listing he came across a match grade Springfield Armory M1A with a number of accessories, including a scope mount. Himes jotted down the information and contacted the seller from his throw away phone. While it may have left a trail, he preferred using it instead of his regular number. At least he could throw that one away without losing all of his other contacts.

The seller was much like Mark: unemployed and running out of options. The only reason he was selling was because he needed the money worse than he needed the rifle. Since the rifle was used, albeit barely, he was willing to negotiate on the price and in the end included 500 rounds of NATO headstamped surplus ammunition from Malaysia and all of his magazines. Both men were smiling by the end of the bartering, one with a rifle and the other with $1200.

Reduction

Mark soon had the rifle in his vise at the shop with the flash suppressor removed and measurements for his next suppressor jotted down on his notepad. He began sketching out the rough plans for the can he would build over the next few days. By comparison it would be larger than the one he built for the AR, but still compact for the size round it would be suppressing. If he built it right he hoped to see a comparable reduction in muzzle blast and sonic signature.

It took three days to work up the first prototype and fit it up to the rifle. Mark had already zeroed the rifle without the can attached a few days earlier using the surplus ammo included in the sale. He figured that it would be more difficult to trace surplus ammo than anything bought off the shelf at the local department store. Using a scope from an older rifle, Mark had doped it to 400 yards and was grouping under three quarters of an inch at that. He decided to field test the suppressor and see if there was any difference in performance. After running a few rounds through the system he was very satisfied, but it was still considerably louder than the suppressed .223 he had already used. He decided to do a little more research and eventually settled on using subsonic ammo which ultimately yielded a consistent 131 decibel crack.

The next couple of weeks came and went without much in the way of work. John kept assuring him that there were jobs coming, but they were working to prioritize and value the targets. Eventually his phone rang and John met him with a stack of folders.

"Take your pick," he said, "We have a broad selection this time. Some pay more, but others are considered more of a priority."

Mark opened the first folder and scanned the arrest record of the individual, then closed the folder and repeated the process with the second. John had tried to include maps and notes wherever possible, but some info was simply not available. Mark browsed each folder in turn and selected the sequence he would follow for each hit. He chose a known child molester as his first target. The man was not one of the most valuable or highest priority, but was toward the top of the list and information was plentiful.

Within the next few days Himes had his location selected and his plan laid out. The target worked a night shift job, but liked to go to a specific park when he got off in the mornings. He would sit and ogle any children that came within sight, but especially focused his attention on the younger, elementary aged girls. His obsession and the abundance of children made his schedule disturbingly predictable. Though he had been taken to court before for crimes against children he had been very thorough and deliberate not to leave a trail. A criminal

Reduction

profiler had been called in to assist the department in the case against him and warned that he clearly fit the mold for a child predator. With the case lost he was free to return to his lifestyle, and his perversion.

Mark left early to arrive at the park before it became too populated and his target got off work. As he set up his shooting position he noticed that his quarry had arrived a few minutes early. The car slowed to a stop and he watched the man step out. In his hand he carried a bag from one of the local fast food chains. Breakfast.

Mark followed him through the scope, occasionally scanning the surroundings for bystanders that might witness the reduction. It was still early enough that there weren't many people stirring about, but it wouldn't be that way for long. Himes decided to make the shot quickly and quietly and move out as soon as possible. He didn't have to wait long. The distance didn't demand the M1A, so he brought the suppressed AR. He snuggled up to the scope and got a solid cheek weld, then scanned the park again.

An elderly couple was slowly making their way around the walking track while a young woman jogged into view from the other direction. Himes checked his target again. He sat on the park bench eating a breakfast sandwich and staring down the jogger that fast approached his position. As she passed in front of him his attention followed her, almost as if he'd forgotten completely about the meal in his hand.

One last scan of the area let Mark know that the time had come. He peered once again through the scope. The target sat slightly bladed to Mark's position with his right side presenting. Mark at first set his sight on the man's head, but decided to drop him with a more subtle approach. The thought of someone's child finding a headless lump sprawled across the bench left him unsettled, so he moved the cross hairs down to the chest cavity. The man's right arm was slightly forward and exposed just enough of the side to allow a well placed shot in.

Himes steadied his breathing and flipped the safety off. He pressed the trigger and the round was away. The target jumped slightly as the round pierced his shirt and embedded into his chest, deflecting slightly downward as it struck a rib. Before he could muster a scream the rifle coughed again and a second round punched through the lung and impacted the heart, shredding the organ and dropping him back to the bench. He sat upright, slightly slumped forward, with the biscuit still in his grasp. The pair of hollow point rounds had done their job and now it was time to go. With any luck no one would notice the man wasn't sleeping for a while and by then Himes would be safely away.

Himes broke the rifle down into primary components of upper receiver, lower receiver and suppressor and tucked them into his backpack. Slinging the pack onto his back he assumed the appearance of a cross training enthusiast and made his way around the track until he could slip away from the park and back to his truck. A quick text later and Himes was on the way home.

Next on his list was a drug dealer with suspected connections to one of the larger inner-city gangs. After studying his dossier he decided that another night operation would be better. Still, he needed to see the area first hand and pick his vantage point. It was farther into the eastern part of town than he had worked before and the problems would be more complicated as well.

Cautiously Mark cruised the area, well aware of all the odd looks he was getting from the people on the streets. Clearly he did not belong and they knew it. To set up a hide in broad daylight would be nearly impossible but to set it up at night could be just as difficult. He preferred to take the shot from a lofty position to minimize the possibility of a bullet passing through the target and traveling on. An innocent casualty was unacceptable, though Mark wondered by the looks he got how many people in the area were 'innocent' at all.

An old public school building showed potential, but the front steps clearly indicated that it was a common ground for homeless or gang members. Just a block or so away from the school sat a run down movie theater. The entrance was boarded shut and there didn't seem to be any signs that it was in use. He decided to look into it closer.

That night Mark returned to the area and carefully made his way to the old theater. He found a side door that was slightly ajar and slowly eased inside. The street lights provided just enough light to see inside the door, but once inside the darkness was total. Concerned about the structural stability of the

Reduction

building Himes thought it best to turn his flashlight on and take a chance at being seen as opposed to falling through the floor. His flashlight was an older model angle head light with interchangeable lenses. He had already swapped the normal, clear lens for the red one to help preserve his natural night vision.

He eventually found the roof access and, to his delight, it was a simple cover over the hole and not a hatch. That would make things much quieter. He climbed onto the roof and low crawled to each side to survey his environment. He finally decided that this would be the best vantage point from which to take the shot. From the info packet he knew his best bet would be a daytime shot, which meant that he'd have to be in position early...again.

Himes told his wife that he would be working an all night assist job and that he'd probably not be home before she and the kids left for school the next day. He left out with his backpack, stopping briefly at the workshop to pick up the M1A and suppressor. He made his way back to the theater and slipped through the side entrance like he had before, then quietly worked his way to the roof. There he would catch some sleep in the early morning hours before going to work.

As the sun broke over the neighborhood Himes could already hear people on the street below. He reached into his pack and produced an MRE for breakfast. Despite the reputation of military food, Mark thought that, overall, they were pretty good. Some, in fact, were very good, especially if you hadn't eaten in a while. Each MRE had its own heater pack that relied on a chemical reaction with water to produce enough heat to warm the meal through and they could get extremely hot. That thought reminded him of a conversation he had a few years earlier with a friend of his.

Reduction

Tommy Jackson had been Himes' friend since elementary school. When they graduated Tommy had enlisted and was eventually deployed to Afghanistan. In the Army he learned that you could use a small amount of water and an MRE heater to make, for lack of a better term, a simple flash bang grenade. Mixing the components in an empty water or soft drink bottle and then quickly capping it caused the bottle to over pressurize and explode with a deafening 'pop.' More a noise maker than an explosive, it was extremely loud and could be mistaken for a gunshot. The problem was that timing was nearly impossible. Perhaps that could be valuable one day.

Movement down the street shook him back into the present as he saw a group of younger men mulling about in front of a known gang hangout. He scanned the crowd through the scope and couldn't identify his man. Some of the youth were indeed bold as he could clearly see them carrying weapons openly

Reduction

in broad daylight. He watched them for a while with the magnification dialed back for a wider field of view when he saw a pair of cars come into view from a side street. The second car matched the description of the target's vehicle according to the info pack from John. Both cars slowed to a stop in front of the group and the doors opened.

Himes realized that a shot through the window would be easy with the .308 rifle round, but he couldn't be sure who was driving due to the glare on the window. Additionally, a window shot would be a clear indicator of the shot's origin. He couldn't risk running in this part of town. He would have to take his time to get away, but still do it as soon as possible.

The range was 670 yards and wind was calm. As the morning warmed the winds would rise and the ballistics would change, complicating the shot.

The driver stuck his head out and partially stood in the door of the vehicle. That wasn't his

Reduction

mark. The passenger door finally swung open as three men approached the car. There he was. He stepped out and engaged the trio in conversation as Himes took aim. The man stepped away from the car and onto the sidewalk. It was now or never. Once he went inside the opportunity was lost.

Himes pressed the trigger and sent the thirty caliber ball downrange, directly into the rib cage of the target. The cavitation was extreme as the shock from the round pulverized internal organs and dropped the individual to the street. He never knew what hit him. Neither did his friends.

Some of them stared in disbelief as others scoured the streets in an effort to locate the shooter. Gunfire began to echo back from the group as some fired indiscriminately in every direction, 'feeling' for him. Himes was about to put his weapon away when he saw a bystander get caught in the melee, dropping to the curb. He had to put a stop to it. Now.

Reduction

Raising his optics again he pulled the trigger and dropped the first gunman who stood behind the dead man's car door. The position made for a perfect head shot and the man dropped instantly as most of his head disappeared in a spray of crimson mist.

The second shooter dove to cover behind a mailbox and began to scan the area, still unsure of where the shots had come from. Estimating his position Himes let loose with a pair of shots into the side of the large blue container and saw the body flop onto the concrete as the rounds found their mark. One buried deep into the chest and the other shattering the hip, sending shards of splintered bone through the femoral artery. Within seconds the sidewalk was covered in blood. Most of them dashed inside the building but the two that remained outside continued to scan the area with weapons raised. Neither fired, but through the scope Himes realized he had been spotted.

Reduction

One of the pair had stepped inside the doorway, giving partial cover from his angle, and was scanning his direction. Mark could clearly see the expression on the man's face as he spotted his position and raised his weapon to fire. Mark squeezed the trigger once more before the gang member could give his position away and sent a 147 grain missile directly into the forehead. The body dropped to the sidewalk like a sack of potatoes.

Himes quickly swung his scope onto the second man and saw that he was already around the corner and running fast. It was time to move. He grabbed his gear and began stuffing items into the pack as quickly as he could, then scooted across the roof to the hatch. Soon he was downstairs and to the side door. Checking his egress he stepped out and headed to the alleyway behind the building. After several tense minutes he heard the sound of sirens en route. A few minutes more and he would be back at his truck. Those minutes seemed like hours, but he finally made it. As he drove home he considered what had just happened and a thought occurred to him. Were any of the others on his list? If not, what would the Chief say?

Early the next morning, as Angie and the kids were making their way to the car, Mark's throw away phone rang. John apparently had seen the results of his handiwork and needed some answers.

"Good morning," Mark said in a tired, but upbeat manner, "I'll bet I know what's on your mind today."

"What the hell happened, man?" John's tone wasn't so much one of anger, but of surprise and confusion, "The Chief has been on the phone with reporters all morning. I'm afraid you're getting famous, Specter."

Reduction

Mark smiled at the thought of the nickname, "Yeah, well, shit happens I guess. You have a chance to meet today? I'd feel better explaining in person."

"Yeah, we have a bit to talk about. Meet me in the mall parking lot in forty-five minutes?"

"I'll be there."

Forty minutes later Mark pulled into the parking lot at the River Glenn Mall, across from the Bass Pro Shop entrance. As he turned the ignition off he saw John's unmarked car circling the area. A few seconds later and the two friends were side by side.

"What's up?" Mark said, as casually as he could muster.

"Chief wants to know what happened. Actually, he doesn't, *want* to know, but he's really, *really* curious. Personally, I just want to know."

"You want the long story or the short one?"

"Make it the short one. I'll get details later if I need them."

"I got my vantage point the night before, slept on the roof and waited for the target to show. He finally showed, I took the shot and his buddies started firing back."

"They see you?"

"Not at first, but they hit a bystander and I felt that it would be wrong not to do something before someone's kid or grandmother got shot by one of those idiots."

"Hmmm," John started, "So you were doing your civic duty by shooting the others?"

"I'm doing my civic duty by shooting the ones you hire me to shoot. Those guys, well, I just thought it best to take them out before anyone else got hurt. Like taking the keys away from a drunk driver."

"So they didn't see you."

"Oh, no, one of the last two saw me I know. He looked right at me and was about to fire when I popped him. If I hadn't he would have had his buddy zero in on me too. I didn't plan on it getting this messy, but, well..." Mark's voice trailed off, searching for a final word but not quite finding it.

"I see. The buddy, did he see you?"

"I don't think so. When I shot the spotter I immediately swung over to pop the sidekick. All I saw of him was assholes and elbows. He was around the corner and gone before I could take the shot."

"Well, the crime scene team worked the place over and hasn't found a single witness who's willing to talk to us about what happened. All we know is that someone shot four people from an elevated position. Family members are raising all kinds of hell with investigators because they are saying that nothing's being done, but when we ask if they have any information they could share every one of them gets suddenly quiet. It's like a friggin' circus sometimes and the clowns are everywhere."

"They know I was elevated? Do they have an idea of the vantage point?"

"The bullet holes in the mailbox indicated a direction, but to be honest they haven't looked hard enough to put the two together. Last I heard the .30 caliber round looked a lot like something fired from an SKS or AK, which is common among the gang members. What has them curious is the number of bodies. Either the dead guys sucked at perimeter defense and security, or the shooter was really good."

"Mind if I ask a question?" Mark prodded.

"Go ahead."

"Were any of the others on your hit parade?"

John laughed quietly, "Here, I've got something for you." He reached over to the passenger seat and grabbed a plain white security envelope, then tossed it to Himes.

Mark opened it up, marveling at the contents, "Holy crap. I take that as a 'yes.'"

Reduction

"The primary was worth $5000, as we already discussed. Two of the three were already on the list for various reasons and the other two were suspects in a gas station robbery from last Monday night. Not bad for a night's work, huh?"

Himes studied the envelope a little longer, "No, I guess that's not bad for a night's work."

Mark took the eleven thousand dollars and tucked most of it away in his workshop. A very small part of it he deposited in the bank to show earnings for the work Angie thought he had done and an even smaller portion he kept as cash to cover his personal and "operational" expenses. Mark was already well past the half way point of the estimated salary he had discussed with John for the work. He wondered if they would stop giving him contracts when the money maxed out or if they would keep sending jobs his way. All he knew for sure was that he would keep doing them until they didn't need him to anymore.

Reduction

When Angie came home that evening Mark had dinner waiting and the deposit already tallied into the account register. After eating and homework had been done the kids disappeared to play video games and play with dolls while the adults caught up on the activities of the day at Angie's work. Angie turned the television on to catch the weather for the next day and settled down on the couch with Mark. First she would have to endure the news, then she could hear the only part of the program she really cared about. There was supposed to be severe weather on the way and she didn't like to be unprepared when it came to storms.

Reduction

The news rambled on with tales of the economy and politics, problems in some of the schools followed up by a sneak peek at the latest investigative reporting dirt. A quick overview of the traffic situation always preempted the weather portion as well, so it would still be a few minutes. Her attention was grabbed by a breaking news headline about a multiple homicide on the east side of town. According to the police the details were still very sketchy, but four people had been shot in broad daylight during a considerable gunfight. Interviews with witnesses and bystanders indicated that the shootout may have been the result of a vigilante.

"Neighbors in the area are condemning the police department for the incident, saying that the shootings would never have happened in any of the more affluent parts of town," the reporter stated, "Representatives of the department have already indicated that some of the victims were, in fact, wanted for various crimes, but declined to go into detail. We'll keep you posted as this story develops."

Mark wondered what was going through her mind, but she didn't seem to have any comment on the subject. Perhaps that was best. Sometimes he wished she would get the weather from the internet or the Weather Channel instead of the local news. Not hearing about some of the things he had done would make keeping it a secret a lot easier.

Over the next few days the news continued following the story and each broadcast the demand for police action seemed to be more intense. Mark called John to see if he could interest him in lunch only to discover that Dahlgren had, in fact, announced an increased effort to find the gunman. The manhunt was on and he would have to be more conscious than ever about watching himself in the field.

Reduction

After a talk with the Chief, John called Mark and told him that they had decided to put any more jobs on hold for a while until the issue cooled off. In the meantime Mark could focus on other items, like the upcoming summer break. He would need to manage his schedule around the kids somehow, since they had decided he would assume the role of babysitter and they could save the cash. The reprieve would also give Mark some extra time to work on developing new tools for his trade.

Chapter 4

John and Mark sat opposite each other at the large layout table in Mark's workshop. Between them, among the coffee cups and candy bar wrappers, sprawled dozens of pages of information. Maps, photos, arrest records and markers littered the space. It had been almost 4 weeks since Mark's last job and the Chief needed him again.

John had warned him that they were still officially looking for a vigilante and that he should be extra careful. Most officers weren't putting any effort into their pursuit, but there were a few that had been described as "crusaders" who longed for the fame and recognition for doing an exemplary job. This added to a growing complexity of Mark's employment.

The problem was that in the week prior some officers had been called to a robbery in progress. As

Reduction

the first unit rolled onto the scene the thieves turned their attention, and their weapons, on the officer.

As they exited the liquor store the suspects opened fire on the patrol car. The officer returned fire, seriously injuring one before taking a round to the forehead. The lucky shot was fired by the accomplice, who fired a nine millimeter. The wounded man was shooting a forty caliber. He would later bleed out on the operating table. The officer was in critical, but stable condition and was recovering from an exhaustive surgery. By and large the entire department was furious over the incident, but the Chief had taken it quite personally.

"The whole department is looking for this guy whenever and wherever they can," Thompson commented, "As a result, all of his known hangouts are under observation. So far nothing has turned up."

"So, what *exactly* are you expecting me to do?"

Reduction

"Chief has authorized you to 'reduce' this individual at any given opportunity. He is currently number one on the hit list. Pardon the pun."

"Uh huh." Mark said as he studied the mug shots again, "and what if I see him on the side of the road while I'm going to the park with my kids?"

"You can always call us. There's a $5000 reward being offered by the department for info leading to an arrest. He's worth $10000 to you dead. You can do the math if you want to. As for me I think I'd be getting to a gun."

Mark sat silently for a minute, considering the information.

"This is the biggest hit we have on the list. We have no idea where he is or where he might turn up. If you get the shot, take it," John added.

"Any suggestions on where I can find him? Anything that isn't laid out here?"

Reduction

"Your guess is as good as mine. We don't think he's left town, but that is a possibility. We figure someone's hiding him out until things cool off and he can get out. Right now the only images we have of him are from the security cameras at the store and stills from that are being circulated at all the bus stops, train stations, airports, cab services, and among all the patrols. If he left, it had to be right after the robbery, before we could identify him. Since the robbery flopped, we figure he's out for easy money. I wouldn't be surprised if he tried another robbery, but so far he's been quiet."

"Alright. I'll keep my eyes peeled," Mark said, "Not sure what I can do that you haven't already done. I'd say the odds are in your favor, but I'll pop him given the chance."

Himes' flat, matter of fact tone struck Thompson with curiosity.

Reduction

"I know I've asked you this before, but are you OK with doing this?"

"Yeah. Why?"

Thompson half grinned, "It's just that you sound really...business like. That's all."

"Well, to me that's what it is. Would you rather I pulled the trigger and then melted into a ball, crying my eyes out?"

"No, no. I don't mean it like that. It's just I don't want you going all '1000 yard stare' on me, you know?"

Mark laughed at the reference, "You've been watching too many Vietnam movies, man. Next you'll be worrying about me hanging claymores in the trees when I go deer hunting."

The two men laughed at the thought, then Himes' smile began to fade.

"You know, John, I've gotta be honest. I actually do kind of enjoy the work." Mark glanced at his friend, his face almost cold, "I don't mean I dream about it or anything, but, well, it's kind of like solving a mystery or something. All the planning and recon, the stealth of getting in and out, the surge of adrenaline when the target's in sight. Then, when all is said and done, there's a sense of satisfaction that everything came together and paid off."

"So, the actual *act* of pulling the trigger and ending someone's life...that doesn't phase you at all?"

Himes sat for a moment considering the question, "Nope. I mean, it's all a matter of perspective. How you look at things. The way I look at it is more from the standpoint of a hunter, I guess. Instead of seeing a person, I see a predator, a parasite. Someone whose livelihood depends on victimizing someone else. When I take the shot, it's more like putting down a rabid animal than killing a person. They serve no purpose other than to take advantage of someone else. It's easy to put them down because I know that someone else won't be their victim. It's not like I'm 'bustin' a cap' in Santa or something."

"OK. I just wanted to be sure. I have to check every now and then. You know, just to be sure you won't snap on me and start popping rounds off in traffic somewhere."

The two friends continued talking about the case at hand until it was almost time for Angie to come home. Mark cleared the table, just in case any curious onlookers wandered in. As he filed the paperwork away John turned the conversation in another direction.

"So, have you looked into any other weapons for your contracts? Anything to help blend in to your environment more?"

"Well," Mark began, " I looked into the SKS, AK, and several different models of 9mm and 40 caliber pistols. I know .38's are common as well, but to be honest I haven't seen anything that gives me the accuracy over distance that I feel comfortable with. You know how much I like the long range shots."

"Have you thought about the possibility of closer range weapons? I mean, there could be a time when you need to use one."

"I have and I don't care for the thought, actually. I feel comfortable with my .45 and I'm pretty good with it, so I've always counted on it for my back up."

John studied the subject a bit more, then added, "Do you have a spare barrel?"

"What, for my .45?"

"Yeah. If you have a spare barrel you can work up one of those 'extensions' like you did for the rifle. That way ballistics won't be able to match your gun to any recovered rounds, if the suspicion ever arose."

Mark considered the approach and thought it had merit. He would begin researching the design that evening from all the information he had already gathered for the other designs. By week's end he would have a prototype that he hoped he'd never need.

Mark picked up a spare barrel online and carried the .45 to the range to check the performance with the new component. He loaded the magazine and proceeded to work his way through the course dropping the steel "pepper poppers" with round after round. He reset the course and added steel plates to the mix. Again, the .45 ran smooth and without issue. Next he moved to the adjacent range where the range was equipped with various barricades and doorways to simulate more of a close quarters environment.

Mark ran the course repeatedly, each time being mindful of the muzzle of the weapon as he tried to allow for the additional length that a suppressor would add. He knew he would need to run the pistol again after threading the barrel and fitting the device

Reduction

to it, but so far he was satisfied with the overall accuracy and operation.

By the end of the day he had shot almost two hundred rounds of 230 grain full metal jacket ammunition through the barrel with only one malfunction. That was directly attributable to the round itself since it apparently had a bad primer. Mark loaded the firearm and remaining ammunition back into the range bag and headed home.

As he worked his way across town he decided to stop and grab a quick lunch. A few blocks away was one of his favorite locally owned burger joints. Himes didn't care much for fast food franchises. The food was usually of poor quality and the prices were always too high for what they sold. Plus it always annoyed him when they asked if he wanted to 'up-size' his meals so they could charge even more.

He preferred the comfortable, almost home-like surroundings of the locally owned restaurants and

Rachel's was one of the best. The burgers were notoriously large and the fries were practically famous around the area. He pulled into the parking lot just as the lunch rush was beginning to thin out and parked beside a brand new Corvette.

"Must be nice to have a steady job these days," Mark muttered to himself as he stepped out of the truck and locked the door.

He swung the door open and proceeded to an open stool at the counter with his mind already made up regarding his order. As he sat down he heard a familiar voice call out from a nearby booth.

"Mark Himes. Long time, no see, man."

Himes turned to see the speaker with a puzzled look on his face, recognizing the voice, but unable to put a face with it. There, just behind him, sat a smiling Joey Davis.

"Well, I'll be," Mark said, "Joey Davis. Where have you been hiding lately?"

"Here and there, man, here and there. How have you been since the shutdown?"

"Getting by. How about you? Find any place worthy of your skills?"

"Oh, I'm doing alright. You check out my ride outside?"

"Hmm? You mean the 'Vette? That's yours?" Mark said with a start.

"Yessir! Ain't it a beauty?"

Mark was stunned. "What kind of work are you doing these days? I don't know of any machinist that can afford a new Corvette for his daily driver."

"Oh," Davis announced, "I'm not in the machine shop anymore. I made a career change. I'm in sales now, and, not to blow my own horn but, I'm pretty good at it."

"Sales? You?' Himes seemed to struggle to digest the notion, "I never would have seen that coming. I gather you like it?"

Reduction

"Oh, yeah. The money is great and the perks are unbelievable. You have to know what you're doing to keep the money coming in, but, well, did you see my car?"

Himes was taken by the announcement and wanted to learn more, but hated to seem prying. He wondered if this might be something he could do. At least it could be a steady job and the money was apparently good, if you were a good salesman.

The waitress took their orders and retired to the drink fountain, leaving the pair alone again. Finally Himes could stand it no longer.

"So, how did you come to be a salesman, anyway?"

"Well, long story short, I was getting frustrated with the whole job hunting routine. I mean everywhere I looked the jobs that were available either weren't for me or I was too old, too experienced, or too highly paid. You know what I mean. Folks would rather hire a kid right out of school for half the wages than someone with tons of experience. Even though it might cost them time and money bringing him up to speed."

Himes nodded as he listened, recalling his own experiences and understanding all too well the frustration of trying to find a job.

"Anyway," Davis continued, "I was talking to a friend of mine one day. My unemployment had run out, my unemployment extensions had run out, the rent was due, the utilities were past due and I was about to give up. I was thinking about just selling everything and moving off to somewhere, anywhere, I might find a job. He told me he knew a guy who was looking to expand his business and he needed sales people. I told him I didn't have any experience in sales and he said not to worry. It was easy and with my personality I was a shoe-in to be good at it. I met the guy, we talked, he liked me and gave me a shot.

Next thing I know I'm bringing in big bucks and the boss is moving me up the ladder."

Himes sat for a moment while the waitress sat their dinks on the table and announced that their meal would be ready soon. Finally he asked the question that had been plaguing him throughout the conversation, "So, is your boss still hiring?"

Davis took a long sip from his glass, then countered, "Uh, no. Right now he's got everyone he needs. Besides, you wouldn't like the guy. He can be really...particular about moving product."

"Aw, man. You remember the kind of crap we had to put up with back in the shop. Every day there was a new deadline or rush job. I could handle it. Who knows, I might be the best salesman he ever had."

Davis laughed, "Well, that's just all the more reason for me not to put in a good word for you then, isn't it?"

Reduction

Himes could tell that the subject of the job was becoming uncomfortable for Davis and decided to lay off the topic to give him a break. He still wondered what kind of company would take such an extreme chance as to hire a machinist with no sales experience to be a salesman. There was definitely something odd about it, but then again, who would have ever dreamt that the police department would be secretly paying a machinist to be a vigilante sniper.

Himes and Davis finished off their burgers and passed the time with idle chat until the waitress returned once again, this time with their checks. She laid both tickets on the table and cleared the plates and glasses away, thanking the pair for their patronage before slipping back toward the kitchen.

Davis quickly reached across the table and snapped up Mark's tab.

"This one's on me. My treat."

"That's really not necessary, man. I may be doing odd jobs to make ends meet, but I can still pay for my burger."

Davis smiled, "Nope. I said it was my treat. Let's leave it at that."

"If you're sure," Himes began, "I don't want to reject your hospitality, but I won't stand for a handout either."

"Not a handout. Just me saying 'thanks' for all the pep talks you gave when the plant was closing down," Davis glanced at his watch, "Oh, I gotta run. I have to meet a supplier in a few minutes. It was good to see you, Mark. Keep in touch, man."

"Yeah, you too. And, if you guys need any more help I'd appreciate it if you'd keep me in mind."

Davis smiled again as he left the register and headed out the door. Himes watched as his former co-worker slid into the leather seat of the Corvette and backed out of the parking space. Questions filled

Reduction

his mind about the encounter and he wondered if there really was a chance that Davis might put in a word for him. Even though he had to admit that he loved the thrill of the work he was doing, it would be nice to not live the necessary double life that went along with it.

Mark returned to the comfortable familiarity of his truck, but he secretly wondered how it would feel to drive a nice expensive car like Davis. The rendezvous stayed on his mind all the way home. When he reached his driveway he checked the mailbox and found the latest copy of *The National Rifleman* magazine among the junk mail and bills. On the front was a massive, full cover photo of the latest Springfield XD series .45 ACP surrounded by hollow point ammunition and tactical gear. Scattered about the image were the titles of various articles contained within the publication, among them was one concerning clandestine weapons of World War Two.

Reduction

Perhaps he could get some inspiration from that, Himes thought.

When Mark got to the house he systematically began to stow his range gear and ammo in their appointed places, then stripped the new barrel from the .45 and relocated to the shop. Once inside he began to modify the muzzle of the component in order to accept the new suppressor. Mark had studied various methods for attaching a silencer to a firearm and found that he liked the threaded barrel approach as opposed to pins or twist-lock systems. Threads were not as quick to attach and detach the device, but he liked the feel of a positive engagement and, though he had no research to prove it, he felt like the tighter threads actually helped reduce sound a bit further.

It took him ten more days to work up the actual device and get an opportunity to field test it. Stepping out to his makeshift range behind the shop, he screwed the suppressor onto the new barrel and loaded the first of several magazines into the grip of the semi-automatic then chambered a round. He said a quick prayer and then squeezed the trigger. With the ear protection on the sound was incredibly diminished. He proceeded to empty the magazine and removed the can.

Once he had the suppressor in hand he tipped it on end and opened a small bottle of drinking water. After pouring a small amount into the breech end and rolling it around liberally, he shook the excess out and then reattached the can to the muzzle. Mark had decided to experiment with the wet / dry concept to see which approach was more effective. According to his research, wet suppressors were mildly more effective sound reducers due to the cooling effect the "wet" agent had on the expanding gasses. Certain mediums seemed to be popular choices, but each had certain benefits and drawbacks. All would have to be replenished eventually, but the thicker the substance the less frequently it would need refilling. Lithium grease was a common choice, but Mark didn't care for the way grease would run and drip when heated. The idea of leaving no traces behind meant that a warm pool of greasy powder residue was out of the question. Water was his preferred choice and if it made enough of a difference he would begin loading out with the new toy on his next job.

He loaded a fresh magazine, took aim with the wet suppressor and fired the first round. Immediately he could tell the difference in volume was diminished, but not nearly as much as he had hoped. He continued to fire until the slide locked back and the last casing fell to the ground. All in all he was satisfied with the new suppressor and barrel combination, but carrying it wet would be difficult. He had to think of a way to wet the device quickly or resort to some type of grease or thick oil.

Reduction

As Mark prepped for the first coat of Tactical Black DuraCoat on the new suppressor his disposable phone rang. He quickly stepped over to the layout table and looked at the screen. He didn't recognize the number, so he ignored the call and went back to work. He wiped the device down to remove any oils or surface contaminants with a strong denatured alcohol and let it dry. Next he reached for a small metal hook and suspended it from a wire he had strung across a makeshift paint booth and then picked up a small airbrush. As he reached for the switch on the small compressor his phone rang again.

Mark put the airbrush down and turned his attention to the phone once again. The number displayed was the same number that had shown the last time. Irritated, Mark ignored the ringing and returned to his project.

He hung the suppressor on the hook and flipped the compressor on to build air pressure while he filled the paint bottle with the paint. The first coat went on quickly and would dry equally fast. While he waited Mark decided that the compressor was no longer necessary since there was adequate pressure to complete the job in the tank. He flipped the switch off and carefully looked the suppressor over. The phone rang again.

"Now you're getting on my nerves," he thought to himself. For a moment he considered not even looking at the infernal device, but decided to give someone a piece of his mind instead. Without even looking at the screen this time, Mark snatched the phone up and answered roughly, "What!"

For a second the line was silent, then Mark heard a slight chuckle.

"And a happy 'good afternoon' to you, too, buddy!" John's voice snapped back, "Catch you at a bad time, did I?"

"Wha...Oh. Sorry about that. I've been trying to get some work done in the shop and some idiot keeps calling every few minutes. I thought you were them again."

Thompson laughed again, "That's alright. I understand. I get those calls a lot too. Say, I have something to talk about with you, ASAP. You free anytime today?"

"I can make time. Where and when?"

"How about Charlie-Q's in a half hour?"

"Make it forty-five minutes and it's a deal."

"See you then." The phone went dead and Mark returned to work. He applied the remaining two coats of DuraCoat without further interruption and then headed for his truck.

Charlie-Q's wasn't a fancy restaurant by any means, but it had the best barbecue in the state and the numerous framed articles, awards, and celebrity photos backed the claim up substantially. As Mark stepped inside and placed his order he noticed that John was already at a booth with a platter of ribs. In a few minutes they had his order up and he eased into the bench seat opposite of his friend and liaison.

"No folder?"

"It's in the car. I didn't want to make a scene."

Mark looked around and was about to comment on how empty the place was when John remarked, "It's a lot of information. Trust me. It would have looked odd with that much paper on the table."

"Fair enough. Can you sum it up?"

"This one job will probably make your annual salary."

Mark stopped eating and looked at his friend. A stunned expression settled on his face as if it was suddenly carved there.

"Excuse me?"

Reduction

"Big job. Kind of a rush, too. The catch is you'll need to do a lot of planning to pull it off. I can help you there, but my schedule is gonna be tough."

"This your four day week?" Mark asked. He was aware that most officers worked twelve-hour shifts in three and four day rotations. John would probably have to work four days and be off three, then next week work three and be off four.

"You got it. Anyway, we have a job for you and it is a multiple objective. You up for it?"

"Maybe. What do you mean 'multiple objective' job?"

"Eight to ten targets. Heavily armed and extremely dangerous. Members of a local gang that is trying to get the attention of some larger, national groups. They have been on a spree lately. If they can impress the big boys with their skills, they hope to become a branch office and get the connections for money, guns, and drugs to expand their territory. It's like presenting a business plan to them."

"I don't have any love loss for folks like that, but I gotta ask, what have they done?"

"Anything from simple possession to murder. The straw that broke the Chief's back was a recent armed robbery. To make a long story short, by the time it was all over they left two in critical condition and three dead, including a twelve-year-old girl who happened to get caught in the line of fire. They got a grand total of $327.50 from the store owner. He got shot in the head point blank."

"I remember that on the news. You got a positive I.D. on all parties involved then?"

"Store surveillance was clear enough to identify six of the gang bangers. Further investigation has led us to identify the individual that planned the robbery. We already have the names of the leader and

Reduction

his second in command and the headquarters is a well known location among the patrolmen."

"So, why do you need me again?"

"To send in officers to arrest them would be a suicide mission. We need a 'long range' alternative to the situation. We happen to know that they are planning a meeting with one of the representatives of the larger gang sometime in the next month. We also know that this meeting won't be taking place at their HQ. They plan on meeting in the warehouse district and, according to our informant this could very well be the meeting that they have been waiting for. If we can eliminate these people we can prevent, or at least postpone, their access to cash and weapons that would give them a significant edge over law enforcement in this area and remove an increasingly violent criminal element from our streets."

"Why do I get the feeling this won't be as easy as it sounds?"

Reduction

Thompson smiled, "Mama didn't raise no fools, huh?" Mark smiled and shrugged his shoulders in modest agreement. Thompson continued, "You're right, though. We're not sure how many will actually be there, but we know these guys and at least a few of the big leaguers will be as well. Without a doubt there will be extra security from both groups."

Mark studied long and hard at the offer. The troubling thing wasn't the number of targets or even the amount of security. It was vantage point. Mark didn't know the warehouse district very well, but he knew that finding a lofty spot with a good field of view was going to be tricky among the large, featureless buildings that populated that part of town. The M1A would give him the rapid follow up needed to address the targets, and enough punch to only need one round each, but he would need to have enough distance to make a clean get away if things went wrong.

Reduction

"Any suggestions or advice?"

Thompson smiled, "I thought you'd never ask. Look here." Thompson produced his smart phone and opened the Google Earth app. Zooming in to the satellite imagery of the warehouse district Mark couldn't help but think how much technology had changed since he was young. That phone had more capability than the first desktop computer he had ever used. Perhaps he would upgrade to one some day.

"I was thinking you could stage yourself on the rooftop of one of theses buildings," Thompson indicated a group of about three large metal structures loosely surrounding some older brick buildings.

"Not a lot of cover up there. What's to keep me from being spotted?"

"Distance more than anything. Our information says they are meeting in this building," John pointed to a large building tightly surrounded on both sides of the main entrance by large steel additions which created a "fatal funnel" effect, a narrow passageway from the parking area to the door. The funnel was no more than 15 feet wide and probably 30 feet long with nowhere to hide. Clearly they had not considered it an issue for security, or had thought it would be a good way to protect flanks while they moved inside.

"I can tell you're thinking the same thing I was. That hallway is a meat grinder, right?"

Mark smiled, "That's just scary. I can see why they might not be worried about it, though." John looked curiously at his friend before Mark continued, "It would be really hard to pull off a drive by with an opening that small to shoot into."

"Hmm. I never thought about that. You could be right."

"My guess is that they think like gang bangers. They fight other gang bangers. That's what their number one opponents would do, so that's who they prepare to defend against. The police aren't supposed to know anything about the meeting, so they shouldn't be a concern and, let's be honest here, I'm not a consideration because I'm just a nut job with a gun that happens to walk into a situation, shoot somebody, then melt into the night." Mark chuckled at the super hero overtone in what he had just said.

"Alright, there, Masked Avenger," John smiled, "You getting a plan?"

"Let me think it over tonight and do some snooping around. I may have an idea that could work. My concerns are still the same, but I think I can work something up. How soon did you say this was supposed to happen?"

"Inside of a month. Basically, it could happen tomorrow or it could happen in thirty days. We may not know until the day it happens, so you'll need to be ready to roll out quickly."

"OK. Let me work on it. I'll get back with you. Anything else?"

"One more thing. Remember the cop killer at the top of the list?"

"Yeah, did you pick him up?"

"No. Not yet. A guy matching his description tried to jack a car after a botched robbery this afternoon. Word on the street is it's him, but nobody's giving him up. Keep your eyes open, because he's moving all over town, trying to avoid setting a pattern. For all I know he could be outside getting ready to rob this place right now."

Over the next two days Mark surveyed the warehouses and support structures in the area, weighing the pros and cons of each potential vantage point against the other. Finally he settled on a lofty older building that provided a direct line of sight all the way into the funnel. From that position he could

Reduction

drop anyone in the narrow confines. Again he would rely on the M1A, but he was concerned about the distance. He knew that the round was capable of accuracy over distances beyond this, but that was usually from a bolt action.

As he sat that evening at his reloading bench it occurred to him that if he could develop a load with a high enough muzzle velocity he might be able to flatten the trajectory enough for the accuracy he wanted. Falling back into research mode he began to surf the internet for ideas. It wasn't long before he found a promising option: sabot rounds. Within a week his order was on the doorstep and he was loading out a batch for testing.

Each .30 caliber round was loaded with a .223 bullet nestled in a plastic sabot sleeve. As the round exited the barrel the sleeve would expand and drop away like a shotgun wad, leaving the smaller bullet to continue downrange. Since the smaller weight bullet was being pushed by the larger powder charge the muzzle velocity and ballistic performance was not something you could find load data on easily. Mark was glad the sabots came with a load sheet in the packaging.

Unfortunately, the one thing Mark didn't like was the consideration that the sabots not be used on a firearm with a flash suppressor. The suppressor could potentially act as a trap for the sabot resulting in a dangerous barrel blockage. It looked as if it would be back to the bolt action for the shot. He hoped that follow up shots would be easy.

Stepping out to the range he set up his chronograph and a sight-in target at 50 yards, then returned to his bench and slid the bolt open on the rifle. Inserting a single round, Mark settled in behind his scope and rested the crosshairs on the center of the target. Exhaling slightly to steady the rifle he pressed the trigger and the round broke through the muzzle with considerable flash and a velocity of over 4000 feet per second. Impressive, but if the shot had to be taken at night the flash would be like a beacon. Mark studied the options he had once again.

He could use the .30-06 with normal ammunition and adjust his point of aim for each shot. He could load out with sabot rounds and hope that he wasn't spotted and the rounds were accurate enough over distance. He could use the M1A and hope that the semi-auto could be effective at the range he was plotting or he could find another vantage point. One closer to his objective.

Needing a break from the frustrations of the range Mark decided to head into town for some lunch. Angie had just gotten groceries the night before, but he couldn't seem to find anything he wanted to eat. Besides getting out would give him a chance to clear his head and step away from the situation a bit. Sometimes a fresh perspective is all it takes to see the solution in front of you. He grabbed his keys and his "go bag" and headed for the door. The small messenger style bag had become his constant companion in recent months and carried his .45, spare magazines, suppressor, a small police scanner, burn phone, a laminated city map, notepad and pen, and a small first aid kit. Everything the covert assassin needed for daily activities.

As he reached the edge of town he decided to make an unorthodox move and eat at one of the fast food chains close by. Perhaps a total change of scenery would help in his quest for a clear train of thought. A few minutes later he sat in a booth near the corner dining on the finest frozen, processed chicken sandwich the place had to offer, which wasn't saying much. Himes considered his situation at the warehouse as he swirled a french fry through ketchup. Barely aware of his environment, "condition white" as

Reduction

John would say, he didn't notice the young man enter through the side door.

The restaurant was relatively busy with a number of patrons circling from tables and cash registers to the drink fountains for refills. Conversations resonated loudly among the various groups represented and so the initial elements of the robbery weren't noticed.

The young man entered the establishment with a somewhat nervous disposition and scanned the dining room quickly before making his way to the first register.

"Good afternoon, sir. Will this be for here or to go?"

"To go...please." A slight smile began crossing his unshaven face as he reached toward the small of his back where a compact 9mm semi-automatic rested. Almost in a single, fluid move the pistol was out and sweeping the room.

Reduction

"Everybody listen up!" The grin became almost an expression of desperate insanity as his eyes widened and the muzzle crossed paths with everyone in the room. The dining room became eerily silent except for a few hushed whispers and gasps.

"Nobody move and this will be over quick. Anybody does something stupid, and it's gonna get messy. Now," he aimed the pistol square at the forehead of the young lady behind the register, "empty the drawer, sweet cheeks, and be quick about it. Everyone else, wallets and watches, credit cards and cash in a pile, over here on the counter. You!" he pointed at a lady at the booth next to Mark, "gather everything up and bring it to the counter. NOW!" The woman, visibly shaken at her orders, began to shake and cry, frozen to the very spot where she sat.

Marks eyes flitted from the man to the woman, amazed at his brazenness and infuriated at the same time. How dare this punk! Mark's mind raced to assess the situation and see if there was anything he could do to take this guy out. The thought kept rushing in that if he could just get to the truck he had all the firepower he'd need to eliminate this problem many times over. Unfortunately, he wasn't in the truck and he didn't bring his go bag in either.

The man swung his pistol over to the woman and screamed at her again, "NOW, DAMMIT! I ain't playin' here!" She shook even harder, tears pouring down here mascara smeared face.

"Hold on, man," Mark said gesturing to calm the man down, "She's scared, OK? I'll do it, just point that thing somewhere else." Mark eased to his feet, not sure of what he was going to do, but sure he had to do something soon.

He made his way from table to table and booth to booth collecting jewelry, wallets, and cash from each patron before heading to the counter. As he reached the pick up counter he glanced to his right to see the man impatiently waiting for the manager to unlock the floor safe and empty its contents. In that instant he realized that the moment was at hand. Placing the ill-gotten booty on the counter he turned to his right and lunged for the man's arm and torso, trying to remember some of the self defense moves he and John had covered from years earlier.

Time seemed to slow as Mark's inertia carried him hard into the man's torso, knocking him off balance. The gun hand swung around trying to engage the mass of Himes' body, but it was too slow to get an effective angle. Mark grabbed the top of the pistol, sweeping it downward and toward the counter as the robber's finger pressed the trigger and a round discharged loudly in the small building.

Mark's hand burned from the heat of the barrel but he tightened his grip as the slide tried to eject the spent casing and cycle the next live round into battery, but failed. Mark stepped slightly to the side, blading himself to the man and brought his knee up while simultaneously pulling the man forward into him, driving his knee deep into the thief's abdomen.

The man coughed deeply, exhaling every ounce of air from his lungs, his grip loosening on the pistol slightly just as Mark adjusted and twisted the pistol backwards in the man's hand. As the handgun wrenched its way backward the trigger guard snapped the man's finger like a heavy duty mouse trap. His head craned back, mouth agape and struggling to utter a scream, but unable to catch adequate breath. The man fell to the floor as Mark wrestled the weapon from his hand and aimed it as his face. His face.

He knew this man. How? Who was he?

Immediately cell phones began dialing 911 and the manager swept through the kitchen door with a roll of packing tape. Grabbing the assailant, a team of people surrounded him and bound his ankles and wrists with several layers of tape, then stood guard over him until police could arrive. Mark retired to the closest booth and laid the pistol on the table. He suddenly felt drained, as if all his energy had been ripped from is body.

A few minutes later the parking lot was awash with flashing lights and sirens as officers scrambled to secure the scene and gather information about what had happened. An officer sat across from Mark, noting details of the events as Mark recounted his actions.

"Seems you're quite the hero today," a voice said as the officer stood up.

"John?" Mark's gaze turned from the man on the floor to his friend.

"How are you doing? You OK?"

A slight smile crossed Mark's face, "I guess so. I just came in for lunch, you know?"

Reduction

"I never thought something like this would shake you up," John said nodding to the figure being escorted to the patrol car.

"I never meant to be this close to the action," Mark scoffed, "Why does he look so familiar?"

"You don't recognize him?"

Mark shook his head, "Should I?"

"That's your man. That's our would be cop-killer. Looks like you've got five grand coming your way, my friend. What do you say to that?"

Stunned at the realization, Mark could only come up with one response.

"Turn him loose and let me get to the truck. I think I'd like the full price for this one."

Chapter 5

"Honey, I'm so proud of you," Angie said as she snuggled up beside him on the couch, "I can't imagine what was going through your mind. You probably saved the lives of everyone in that restaurant."

Mark just sat there. Silently considering the events of earlier that day. Not quite sure what to say; not really quite sure of how he felt. He was glad to have stopped the man, to be sure, but something disturbed him deeper down about the encounter. He couldn't help but think about how much more he could have used the full bounty. Was he actually more worried about the money? Maybe it was time to talk to John. Clearly his perspective was changing.

"Mark?" Angie sat beside him, curious as to his silence, "Sweetie, you okay?"

"Hmm? Oh, yeah. Sorry. I guess I'm still a little shaken, you know?"

"I can understand why. I mean, it's not everyday that you just take a criminal out like that." She draped an arm around her husband, trying to reassure him that he was a good man and that he should be as proud of his actions as she was.

Mark smirked at the irony of his wife's comment. If she thought he had done the right thing by catching this criminal, what would she think about his regular source of income?

The pair sat there on the couch for a while, Angie snuggled up to her new found hero and Mark lost in thought. Both kids burst into the room, disturbing the silence and demanding the attention of their parents.

"Back to reality," Angie said as she eased from the couch and headed down the hallway.

Reduction

Ashley, the older of the pair, bounded over to her father and plopped down beside him. She gave him the biggest bear hug she could muster, kissed him on the cheek, and headed for the kitchen. As she reached the doorway, she turned and faced him. With a beaming smile she said, "Daddy, you're awesome. Thank you for not getting hurt though." With that she disappeared into the next room.

Andy watched his sister leave before turning his attention to Mark and decided it was his turn to express his feelings for his dad as well. Crawling up into his dad's lap, he grabbed him around the neck and squeezed tight.

"I like you, I love you, Daddy," he said, almost in a whisper, "I'm gonna go get some cookies, before Sissy eats them all." He slid from Mark's lap and rushed to the kitchen.

Himes broke a smile as he watched them. They were his world. While he shuddered at what

Angie would think about his latest line of employment, he couldn't fathom what the kids would think. After all, it wasn't something you could talk about in polite company, let alone at school for Career Day.

Mark found sleep that night somewhat elusive as his mind continued to replay the robbery over and over. He couldn't help but think of how easily things could have gone wrong. Instead of lying there in bed with his wife on his shoulder, he could have been in the morgue. Finally exhaustion won out and Mark sank into a fitful sleep around three in the morning.

The next day was filled with more mundane activities punctuated by the occasional congratulatory phone call. While Mark appreciated the numerous pats on the back from friends and family, it only served to distract him from his planning. He had finally settled on a structure and a weapon system for the gang meeting. He would use the M1A from a smaller, older building with what appeared to be an elevator house toward one corner. The vantage gave him a clear shot at the "fatal funnel" but from a lower elevation. Mark worried that it might be enough to offer cover behind a vehicle where they could return fire. That brought up the second issue with the location.

Himes had hoped for a long range solution. While the building was still beyond the range of lesser skilled shooters, it was less than half of the over 800 yards he had hoped for. If he were spotted, which he had little doubt he would be before it was over, getting out could be problematic at best. By relying on the semi-auto he hoped to reduce the amount of time he would be shooting and thereby the opportunity to be spotted. His shots would have to be not only accurate, but fast.

John called around mid afternoon to see how his friend was doing.

Reduction

"How are you feeling, superman?"

"Oh, you know, just another day. What's up?" Mark considered talking to his friend about the bounty he'd missed out on. How he seemed to be more concerned about the money than the taking of a life. He decided that it was what it was: business. Pure and simple.

"Chief wants to give you a little something today. Get your spiffy clothes on and comb your hair. It's time to get paid."

"What? Man, I don't want my picture in the paper. Can't you get me out of this?"

"I'm afraid not. This little event is when you get your reward for being a model citizen. Plus, it also gives the department a positive image and, hopefully, will lead to more folks coming forward to help solve crimes."

Mark sat quietly on the phone for a moment before reluctantly grumbling, "Yeah, I guess, but I don't want my picture in the paper. I like my privacy, you know?"

"I know, I know. Look, don't think of it as a booster for the department. Think of it as a way to make *my* job easier. How does that work for you?"

"Fine. What time do I need to be there?"

"Four o'clock. Sharp," Mark could hear the smile crossing his friend's face.

"Fine. I'll do it, but under protest."

John laughed a little before popping his final jab into the conversation, "Oh, and I wouldn't worry too much about having your picture in the paper. You'll be way too busy talking to the reporters from the T.V. stations. See you at four."

Mark was speechless. This was the last thing he wanted to do.

Reduction

Mark strode up the steps to the front doors of the police department. As he opened the door he saw the camera crews setting up their equipment for his network debut. He quietly made his way to John's desk, trying not to look significant. Before he could make the relative safety of his comrade's office Chief Dahlgren and a small caravan of press rounded the corner at the opposite end of the hall.

"Excuse me! Are you Mark?" the Chief called to him. The tone of his voice hinted at a hopeful desperation. Perhaps the press was getting on the Chief's nerves. Maybe that simple fact would speed the whole presentation along and it could be a little less uncomfortable for both of them.

"Um, yeah. Yes. Sir. Chief."

"Good. Good. It is nice to meet you, Mark. Ladies and gentlemen, this is the man of the hour. If you all will step over here, we'll get this underway."

Reduction

The mass of media moved to their respective places among the microphones and tripods. Mark joined the Chief to one side of the mic stands where they were soon joined by John and a couple of other officers that he had met before, but couldn't recount their names.

The reporters gathered around with microphones and recorders aimed at the assembly of men before them, ready at last to announce some good news for a change. Dahlgren stepped to the stand and gestured for Mark to join him up front. As he did so the older man began to speak.

"Ladies and gentlemen, it is my pleasure to introduce to you a true hero to this community. Recently, as I'm sure you all know, a violent robbery attempt was foiled at one of our local establishments. That individual is the same man that assaulted and critically injured one of this city's finest officers in a separate robbery a few weeks earlier. Thanks to incredible pressure form the men and women of this department in their search for him, he made a mistake. His mistake, coupled with the unquestionable bravery of this man, Mark Himes, led to his safe capture."

He turned to Mark and extended his hand, "Mr. Himes, thanks to you we were able to safely apprehend a violent man and make the streets of our fine city just a little safer. We are indeed in your debt. As you know, that debt carries a reward of $5000, and it is my pleasure to present this check to you for your help in apprehending this individual."

Mark smiled as he reached out for the slip of paper, still remorseful that it wasn't for the full bounty, but it was still more than he had before.

"Let's hang on and let them get a couple of shots, OK?"

"Sure. That's what I'm here for." Mark smiled as he shook the Chief's hand among the camera flashes.

In a few minutes it was all over and the press began to dissipate. John stepped up with a grin and began prodding the reluctant hero. Within a few minutes the pair had made their way to the sanctuary of John's office where the subject matter quickly changed.

"How's the planning going?" John asked pointedly.

"I think I have it all worked out. I'm going to have to be careful, though. It's not the setup I would prefer, but I think I can make it work. Any word from your man on the inside?"

John shifted back in his seat and rubbed at his chin, "Well, that's why I wanted to ask. Our information says it will be happening this weekend. Saturday, actually. We've pulled some strings and confirmed that there are about six members of one of the larger gangs coming in Saturday morning. The meeting is supposed to take place that afternoon around 3:00. You should try to be in place well before then to avoid suspicion. What's your hide location?"

Mark pulled out a pencil and grabbed John's notepad, tearing off a sheet of paper and quickly scratching out a diagram of the area. Pointing at a small square on the drawing, Mark told John of the plan and expressed his concerns for being spotted and egress.

"If I get spotted and can't get the shots off, I'm going to be hard pressed to get out clean. I mean, I've got some distance, but I also have multiple stories to climb and a bit of a run to my vehicle."

"I'll see what I can do to get a couple of units in the vicinity to give you a distraction and also to roll in and mop up."

"Just be sure they aren't too close and aren't any of those 'crusaders' you mentioned before. I don't want to be picked up or get them in a crossfire situation." Mark was still very unsure about the setup and adding officers to the mix didn't make him any more comfortable.

Mark folded the paper and tucked it away in his pocket before standing with a stretch.

"No traces, right?" Mark asked his friend.

"No traces."

Soon Mark was on the way back to his house and his mind was occupied with thoughts of the impending job. Before he knew it he was pulling in to the driveway. He needed to get back to the shop and start putting things up before the family got home. That's when he saw that his timing was off. Angie and the kids were already home. Anxiety took over as he hoped that neither she nor the kids had gone to the workshop to look for him. He quickly parked his truck and headed for his shop.

Opening the door he scanned the table, relieved that most of the items he had already put away before going to the press conference. He snapped up the few incriminating items and began putting them away when a familiar voice sounded from the doorway.

"Hey, sweetie. I thought I heard you come home," She slipped in the doorway and hugged him tightly from behind, "How was your day?" She smiled as if she already knew the answer to the question, but he would indulge her with an answer anyway.

"Oh, you know, same old thing. Some machine work, quick trip into town, press conference with the Chief of Police and a run to the bank to deposit the $5000 reward check for being a model citizen. Just another typical day." He smiled as he turned to face his wife. It was strange, in a way, that she had a natural ability to dissolve all the stress from an otherwise uncomfortable situation. Her mere presence was enough to make him relax and suddenly the afternoon wasn't so bad. That was one thing he loved about her.

She lifted her arms to his neck and pressed her lips to his. Mark's mind raced with thoughts of his wife. He knew that she loved him as much as he loved her and this brief moment served to cement the fact firmly in his mind.

The thought suddenly manifested; should he tell her what he'd been doing? Absolutely not. He couldn't risk it. Not even to her. If word should get out it could be disastrous for not only him, as a vigilante, but the police department as well. It would no doubt be the end of Dahlgren's career, and the beginning of countless lawsuits. No. The secret would have to remain between him and John.

"Hey, dinner's almost ready. Are you hungry?"

"Starved."

"Good," she headed toward the door, "By the way. I got a call from mom today. She wants to come for a visit this weekend. I told her it would be OK. I hope you don't mind." She finished her statement with a sheepish grin.

Marks smiled back, "No. No problem at all." He watched her close the door, then turned to put the last of his research material away. That's when it dawned on him.

"Oh, crap."

The remainder of the week came and went faster than Mark had hoped. He had detailed his plan and committed it to memory for the "turkey shoot," as John had referred to it. He would leave out before first light to gain his vantage and conceal himself as best as possible. John had followed up on his hide location and verified that the building would indeed be empty and civilian activity should be minimal at most in the area. All that was left to do was pull the trigger and get back home.

Mark stepped into the living room where Angie was watching television. Her parents were due to arrive in the morning a few hours after he planned on being in the warehouse district.

"Honey," Mark began, "I hate to interrupt Bones and everything, but I wanted to let you know I'll be gone before your parents get here tomorrow."

She muted the program and gave him a curious look, "Is something wrong? I thought you said there wasn't a problem the other day."

"No, no. Nothing wrong. I just forgot that John asked me to go with him and scout some new hunting locations. He is wanting to get a little more involved in hunting to offset his grocery bill. You know, like we've been doing. I figured the best way to do it would be to get him out early and let him have the full experience. I'm going to take my rifle also, just in case we have time to run by the range afterward, but I shouldn't be gone all day. He knows we have company coming."

"Mmm hmm," she smiled, "are you sure you're not just trying to get away from 'the in-laws' before they arrive?"

He smiled back at her, like a child with his hand in the cookie jar.

"Wouldn't dream of it. You know how much I love hanging out with your dad."

"Yeah, yeah. What time will you be leaving?"

"I'm going to leave here around 3:30. I'll have my cell, but I probably won't have a signal since we're going to be pretty deep in the woods. If you need me leave a voicemail and I'll call back as soon as I have a chance."

Reduction

"You going to bed now, I suppose?"

"Yeah. If I expect to roll out that early I need my beauty sleep."

With a quick kiss he was off to bed. He hated to lie outright to her, but he had to have an excuse to get away.

After a fitful sleep Mark slipped out of bed and gathered his gear for the day ahead. He quietly made his way to the truck and headed into town. By the time he was at his pre-determined parking spot it was a couple of minutes after four. He slipped his duffel bag over his shoulder and began the walk to his hide location. The hike was just under a half-mile followed by a short climb up an exterior roof access ladder to the small elevator mechanical room. The room looked to be a frequent hideaway for employees as the interior was littered with empty bottles, candy wrappers, and a few porno magazines and newspapers.

Once inside he strung a sheet of black mesh screen across the open doorway to reduce visibility into the room from outside. He would take his shots from behind the screen to help reduce the muzzle flash as much as possible. A little trick he picked up from watching the Military Channel. The only concern he had was the size of the room. Shooting a large round like the .308 would be deafening in the confines of the structure. He decided to double up on the hearing protection, using plugs in his ears and muffs as well. While it would restrict his ability to hear anyone sneaking up on him, he felt reasonably comfortable that the area was secure enough for his work today.

He threaded the suppressor onto the M1A, loaded the first of three magazines he brought and scanned the area through the scope. Confident that the range was good and the trajectory was clear he settled back in the tiny room and ate breakfast. Within a few minutes the sausage and egg biscuit was history. The sun rose over the warehouses with little life except for a few birds and the occasional stray cat a few buildings over.

Around 8:00 Mark thought he heard an approaching vehicle, its sound system thumping loudly, echoing through the empty avenues below. He peered through the scope intently, finding the car as it cruised slowly by the designated meeting house. It didn't stop. Mark surmised that it must be a scout sent to make sure the area was clear before the big dogs arrived.

About an hour later another car entered the neighborhood, this time a bit quieter. It circled the building where the meeting was to take place and then stopped to the side. A grungy looking duo emerged and approached the doorway, stopping short and assuming flanking positions. The first security detail had arrived.

Next came an Escalade with massive rims that dispatched about four additional figures that took a similar posture around the entrance to the building. Each of the assembled six sported a weapon of various design. Two AK's, one AR, one that looked to be an Uzi or MAC and two carried handguns. They scanned the nearby corridors restlessly as a third vehicle came into view. A Corvette.

"No freakin' way," Mark muttered under his breath.

The Corvette stopped and the driver got out. Through the scope Mark could clearly see the face of his former co-worker and friend, Joey Davis.

"Son of a...," Mark's mind raced with possible resolutions to the situation. He couldn't shoot his friend, could he?

Reduction

He grabbed his cell phone and scrolled through the contact list. There, among all of the numbers he had gained over the years was Joey's. He had to talk to him. Mark hoped that the number was still good and pressed the SEND button as he returned to the scope.

Joey was busy talking to the thugs at the entrance, acting as if it were a gathering around the water cooler at work. Suddenly he reached to his belt and produced a phone. Mark's mind raced. What would he say?

"Joey." the gangster said.

"Hey, man. Mark Himes. You busy?"

"Hey, Mark! Um, yeah, actually I'm a little busy at the moment. Can I call you back?"

"I just had a quick question about your job," Mark stammered for a moment, "You still liking what you do?"

"Absolutely, brother. Um, look, I'm getting ready to meet with some pretty important clients in just a minute. I really need to let you go."

"Oh, I understand, man. Uh, one more question. Would you ever consider another line of work?"

"It's all about the money, man. If something better comes along, I'd be open. Until then, this is what I do, you know?"

"Yeah."

"Look, man, I really need to go. I'll catch you later."

The phone went dead as a silver Mercedes pulled up and parked directly in front of where the men were assembled. Behind it was a black Chrysler 300. The engines cut off and three more men emerged from each car. After a brief exchange of pleasantries the entourage began to migrate toward the doorway. Mark steadied his breathing and adjusted his aim.

The rifle barked and Joey dropped to the ground, a crimson spray lingering momentarily where he stood. Mark adjusted his aim and pressed the trigger again. The second round struck the man directly to Joey's right just below the chin, severing the spinal column and dropping him to the ground like a bag of rocks. Mark swung slightly to the left and aligned the sights with the next victim's head.

Pressing the trigger again the round raced downrange until finding its mark in the center of the man's chest, slightly to the left of center where the kinetic energy ruptured the heart like a heavy water balloon. As quickly as possible, Mark realigned his rifle.

The half-second flight time of each round gave Himes enough time to adjust his aim before the rounds impacted their targets in the narrow corridor.

Since the field of view was so wide through the scope, he was able to confirm each shot while turning his attention to the next.

Through the cross hairs he could see target number four swing up with a small AK and begin sweeping the area with erratic gunfire. As Mark pressed the trigger a fifth man stepped behind the fourth, apparently trying to reach the safety of the building. The round blasted from the suppressor with a loud cough, speeding toward the building and finding its mark.

The round entered the right side of the shooter's neck, slicing the jugular vein cleanly before carrying on and embedding deeply between the shoulders of the fifth man. He collapsed to the ground, twisting momentarily before his brain realized that the spinal column was destroyed. The shooter's hand convulsed as he fell, gripping the trigger and discharging rounds indiscriminately about the narrow hallway and narrowly missing another of the thugs.

Mark moved the cross hairs to the opposite side of the opening in time to fire two more shots at a pair running toward the doorway. The lead man spun to the side and fell against the wall as his left kidney exploded in a spray. His pursuer dropped immediately behind him when the next .308 round burrowed through his left lung, taking a sizeable piece of chest muscle out as it exited.

With no cover in the narrow passage, the remaining men hustled toward the cover of the cars. One fired randomly over the hood of the Mercedes with his AK blindly pointed in Mark's general direction. A second man was behind the trunk of the car, popping his head out and trying to locate Mark. He would time his observation with the AK gunfire in hopes that he could have some degree of covering fire. No such luck.

Reduction

With the next volley the man peeked above the trunk only to be greeted with a 147 grain bullet slamming into his forehead. Immediately another face slipped from behind the bumper, opening up with the AR Mark had noted earlier.

He was pretty sure that none of the men knew his location, but some of the stray rounds were beginning to impact the main building he was using. Mark's adrenaline began pumping overtime as he switched his attention to the Chrysler. The remaining three men were there, but none was returning fire. Finally, the AK stopped chattering and he realized they were working on a plan. Time to put a stop to it, Mark thought. This is taking too long.

Hoping that there was some truth left in Hollywood, he opened fire at the approximate location of the fuel tank on the 300. Three rounds into the side of the car yielded a mad blast from the front of the Mercedes as the AK gunner let his opinion be known. Five rounds in and he struck gold.

The tank erupted in a violent explosion, sending burning fragments of the vehicle in every direction. From behind it, through the smoke and flames, Mark could see two of the three men, bathed in flame, crawling away as if distance would save their lives. Both collapsed mere feet from the wreckage with no more movement. Mark suddenly realized that the AK and AR had stopped firing and swung his attention back to the Mercedes. He could see the muzzle of the AK bobbing slightly above the fender of the sedan and considered taking a shot, but decided that the engine block would be too formidable at that range.

Finally, the last pair made a bold stand. The AR opened up wildly and the man with the AK bolted for Joey's Corvette. Mark led him slightly and fired, but the now hot barrel of the M1A was becoming increasingly less accurate over the nearly 400 yards. The round impacted high and right, missing the escapee by nearly a foot. The semi-auto belched another round and caught the man just as he dove behind the exotic sports car, catching him squarely between the ribs and tearing through both lungs and the heart with one blast. He was dead before hitting the pavement.

Having witnessed the demise of the AK gunner, the last man standing kept himself hidden behind the Mercedes, waiting, wondering how death would come for him. He didn't have to wait long as Mark tried his luck with the second fuel tank. This time it only took two rounds and the car was fully engulfed.

Mark scanned the killing field before him, any movement was met with a kill shot, with one exception.

Reduction

He quickly tapped out a message to John and gathered his gear. The entire incident took less than three minutes and forty-five seconds. He could already hear sirens heading his way as he rushed to the access ladder. Once on the ground Mark began making his way back to the truck. The walk out seemed to be much farther than the walk in early that morning and the sound of sirens kept getting louder with each step. Mark was beginning to worry that he might not make it when he realized he was practically running. He needed to slow down and relax. Running would draw attention and that was one thing he could not afford. He reached the truck and shoved his duffel bag in just as two patrol cars flew by.

As casually as he could, Mark left the area, stopping only long enough to text John once more, then headed directly home. The adrenaline was coursing through him and keeping a tranquil appearance was painfully difficult. Turning onto his road, Mark decided he needed to calm down and get his composure. He pulled onto a side road where he could do just that. For several minutes Mark sat in silence. He suddenly began to shake and felt exhausted. A wave of nausea rushed over him as he pushed the door open and vomited.

"Glad I didn't do *that* in the driveway," he muttered.

Mark sat back in the seat of the truck and took a deep breath. He wanted to scream, or cry, or...something. The emotions of the adrenaline rush were pouring over him like a waterfall. He had never felt such an uncontrollable emotional experience before, but, then he had never had such an emotionally charged day before. After about forty-five minutes Mark started the engine and turned toward home. As he drove he drank the last bottle of water from his duffel in an attempt to rinse the vomit from his breath. No traces meant no traces at home as well.

Reduction

As he pulled in the driveway he decided to stow the duffel bag first in his workshop then let Angie and the kids know he was home. That would give him a couple of extra minutes to cool back off as well. He grabbed the bag and strode toward the shop at a brisk pace. Just as he reached the door he noticed he was being followed.

"Hey there, Mark! We were wondering when you'd be home!"

Angie's father was making quick time across the back yard even as Mark was opening the door.

"Hey, David! How's it going?"

Mark slipped the bag inside the door and quickly locked it back as he turned to face his father-in-law.

"Oh, pretty good. Angie said you had a prior commitment this morning. I wasn't expecting you back for a little while yet. Everything go OK?"

"Fine. We managed to get a couple of spots scouted out this morning before we had to come back to the real world."

"Need any help putting your things away?"

"Nah. I'll sort it all out later. Right now I'm starving and a bit on the tired side. I think I want to go relax in my chair and eat a bit of lunch. Care to join me?"

"How can I resist an invitation like that? The girls are already working up some burgers and fries as we speak," the older gentleman said, "By the way, are you feeling alright? You look a little pale."

Mark smiled, "I'm fine. Just need a little sleep, that's all."

After a short nap in his favorite recliner, Mark awoke to discover that he had slept almost all afternoon. Angie, the kids, and her parents were all curiously absent and the volume on the television had been turned down to the point it was barely audible.

Reduction

Mark rose from the chair and made his way to the kitchen where he spotted a note on the counter.

Gone to Burger King. Be back later. Call if you want us to pick something up for you, sleepy head.

Love,

Angie.

Mark smiled and thought about the offer. He hated fast food, but he could really go for something right about now. He returned to the living room and found his phone on the table by his former bed. He called Angie and placed an order for a chicken sandwich of some type or another, "You know what I'll eat," was all he could give for an order since he wasn't familiar with the exact menu items.

It would be a little while before they returned, so Mark set about to square his gear away in the workshop. When he started clearing the duffel bag out he took a quick glance at the burn phone. John had tried to call him twice and texted him once. That was nearly three hours earlier.

Call me ASAP. We have issues.

Issues? What issues? Mark's mind raced through the egress from the mechanical room. He'd policed up all the spent casings and noone had seen him leave the structure. He had double checked the scene before packing up and made sure none of the gang members were still alive. Even if they had been he was positive they couldn't have seen him from that distance. There was only one issue he could think of.

John answered the phone almost immediately.

"Hey man, I got your message. Is there any time we could get together this evening? I'm a bit tied up right now with work."

"Uh, tonight won't work very well for me. If you have time tomorrow I can probably catch you then. Tell you what, I'll text you in the morning. We can set a time and place then. How would that work for you?"

"That'll work. I'll talk to you then."

The tone in John's voice told Mark that he was probably in the middle of a meeting about the warehouse shootings. He knew that the heat would be turned up considerably, but that came with the job. John wouldn't have bothered about that. Could someone have seen him? The answers would have to wait until morning. The worst part was that it would plague him all night long and he was already running on a sleep deficit.

Early the next morning Mark's phone rang. Angie and the kids had barely closed the door and John was calling.

"Good morning," Mark answered.

"Hey, man. You free today? I wanted to return your call from yesterday. Sorry I couldn't talk then, but work was kind of busy, you know?"

"Oh, yeah. I've seen the news. Looks like you guys had your hands full."

Mark understood by the terminology and tone that John was using that he must either be in the office or around other officers. He wasn't as comfortable in his dialog as if he were alone.

"Yeah, that's an understatement. Can you meet me in, say, a half-hour?"

"Sure. Where?"

"You pick it. I'll be there."

"I'll meet you at the BP station at Fifth and Howard. That ought to be about halfway. Will that work for you?"

"I'll be there. See you in a bit."

Mark hung up the phone and grabbed his go-bag. Within a few minutes he was waiting for John at the market. He didn't have to wait long as John pulled into the spot beside him and stepped out of his Jeep. He looked at Mark and pointed to the store, indicating that he was going to grab a drink or snack before commencing their conversation. Moments later he emerged and sat in the passenger side of Mark's truck.

"You not working today," Mark asked, noting that Thompson was wearing jeans and a tee shirt rather than his uniform.

"Today was supposed to be my day off. Chief thought it would be a good idea to get the details on yesterday from a 'reliable' source, so he called me in. Needless to say, I couldn't tell him anything because I hadn't talked to you."

"Sorry, man. I didn't mean to get you into trouble."

"No, no. I'm not in trouble. As a matter of fact I think he was a bit relieved that I *didn't* know anything. Makes it easier on him for the media. Plausible deniability."

John sat for a second, taking a huge bite from his Butterfinger before continuing, "Let's go for a ride. You got a few minutes?"

"Sure. Where do you want to go?"

"I don't care. Somewhere out of town. A road less traveled," he grumbled, straining to swallow.

Mark pointed the truck toward the city limits and soon they were riding the back roads of the county like he did back in high school.

"So, what 'issues' did you want to discuss?" Mark asked the question, not sure if he really wanted to know what could have gone wrong.

"First off, how many bad guys did you count before firing your first shot?"

"Thirteen. Why?"

"OK. We had twelve dead and one wounded, so they are all accounted for. There was some concern that a couple may have gotten away. Did you see anyone else in the area?"

"Yeah, there was a donk that cruised through about an hour before the main group showed up, but they didn't stop. I figured they were a security detail checking the place out. They never came back."

"OK. We'll look into that. The one survivor is my main concern. Before he lost consciousness he only said one thing; your name. We checked his personal effects. I got his cell. Care to guess who's number was the last call he received?"

Mark wasn't sure if he was in trouble or not. He pulled over to the shoulder of the road and began to plead his case.

"I called him. His name is Joey Davis. I used to work with him at my old job and he's always been a stand up guy. I ran into him recently and he was telling me about this great job he had and all the money he was making. I never thought about someone like him being a dealer...until I looked through the scope yesterday morning."

Thompson studied his friend's face for a minute. He had known Mark long enough to be sure he had meant no wrong by calling the man, but the call had now implicated Mark. If not to the shooting, then to the drug trade. This would have to be sanitized quickly and quietly.

"Why did you call him? What did you say?"

"I couldn't kill him. I was trying to give him a chance to justify himself. To give me a reason not to gun him down like the rest of them," Mark could feel the stress of the event coming back. He had to get himself back under control, "I asked him if there was anything that would make him leave his work. As far as he knows, I think he's a salesman."

"Oh, he's a salesman alright. He's becoming one of the biggest dealers in the city," John interjected.

Mark was stunned for a moment, "Yeah. Anyway, I asked him if there was any way he would consider changing jobs. If he said no, I had already made my mind up that I would drop him like a rock, no matter how hard it was. But he didn't. He said if the right offer came along he would gladly change."

"So you blew his shoulder out rather than kill him."

"Hey, that's what friends are for," Mark managed a sheepish grin, but only for a second, "I figured if I opened his eyes to the danger he was in, maybe that would make him want to get out of it. What kind of shape is he in?"

"He's stable. He's been out pretty much since the ambulance brought him in. He lost a lot of blood, but he should survive. My concern is clearing you of any involvement. I think that should be easy enough. You called about an innocent sales job. He didn't have time to talk about it. After the phone call somebody shot him, and twelve others, in an incident of gang on gang violence. Simple. I still have one question that's been really bothering me."

"What's that?"

"How the hell the did you blow up the two cars? You using some 'special' ammo on this one?"

Mark chuckled, "Nope. I saw it on television. Seems that if you get lucky you can actually shoot a gas tank and it will explode. It took me several more shots to do it than it does in the movies, though."

"We were wondering what set those off. The wreckage was so scattered and everything was burned so badly that forensics is going to have one hell of a time sorting through it all," John smiled at his friend, "You OK?"

"Yeah, I'll be fine. This one just got to me a bit. Seeing Joey through the scope kind of shook me up. I was hoping that I didn't kill him, but I wasn't sure he would make it. That's why I sent the second text. Try to get him ambulatory and stable. Jeez, he was my apprentice at the plant. It's almost like shooting a relative."

Mark ran his fingers through his hair and exhaled sharply, trying to manage his emotions despite the growing urge to break down.

"Do you think it might be possible for me to see him?"

"I'll see what I can do."

Chapter 6

John called Mark around 10:00 and had him come to the hospital. It had been three days since the shootout in the warehouse district and his friend and former co-worker had finally regained consciousness. In the mean time Mark had been interviewed twice by detectives to ascertain his association with Joey. They had checked his story about working together in the plant and were satisfied as to his innocence in the whole situation. It would have looked bad to have the city's recent hero involved with the local gangs, so it was important to make sure he wasn't. The long term friendship also furthered the distance to him being the possible trigger man. After all, what possible reason could he have to shoot his friend and former apprentice?

Reduction

They stepped into the room together with an officer standing watch outside the door. As Mark neared the bed he saw a smile, weak though it was, cross Joey's face.

"What's up, man? You didn't bring me any flowers?"

Mark smiled, "You'd just try and eat them. How are you feeling?"

Joey struggled to sit up a bit more, his shoulder wrapped tightly with bandages and various tubes protruding from his body. Mark thought that he looked somewhat like a Borg from *Star Trek: The Next Generation*.

"I'm feeling OK, all things considered," He cleared his throat and continued, "How are you these days?"

"Pretty good. Still doing the odd job from time to time, but we're managing."

Reduction

Joey thought about the phone call and looked at his friend. His expression changed and he glanced over at John. Mark caught the glance and reassured his co-worker.

"Have you two met? Joey, this is John Thompson. John, this is Joey Davis," Mark turned his attention to Joey, "John and I have been friends for a long time. He's the one who told me you were in here. As a matter of fact, he's the one who cleared it for me to come today. He's a good guy."

"We've never been 'formally' introduced, but, yeah, we've met." Joey looked like a kid that wrecked his father's car. "Um, about your call the other day…"

"Yeah?"

"I've been thinking a lot and, uh, I might be ready for a career change."

Mark looked over his shoulder at John who stepped toward the door and quietly closed it.

"I thought you might."

Reduction

"So, I didn't want to tell you what I was doing for a living when I ran into you that day. Truth be told I knew you wouldn't like it and that bothered me. When you called the other day," Joey again stared at the sheets, conscious of the many wires and tubes monitoring his condition, "I was about to help make a massive deal to bring in one of the bigger gangs and secure a major drug supply line. The money was going to be insane."

For a moment he seemed to be struggling with how to put his feelings into words.

"Then, out of nowhere, I felt this hot blast just slam into me. I felt like I'd been hit by a truck. The next thing I know, I'm laying on the ground and all I can hear is gunfire. Everything was spinning and just before I blacked out I saw DeShawn fall right in front of me. His eyes were wide open, but they didn't move, like he was looking through me or something. That's the last thing I remember."

Reduction

Mark looked at John. Joey hadn't spotted him or even seen where the shots came from. Good news for Mark, and it had apparently had the effect he wanted to get Joey back on the right track. A plan began to form in Mark's mind that would push this to everyone's advantage.

"Joey," He sat back in his chair, almost in a stately manner, "you said you were ready for a career change. Are you serious about that?"

"Man, I'd go back to slinging burgers like in high school if I knew it would mean I wouldn't get shot at again. This sucks."

Mark looked at John again, a slight grin forming on his face. John looked confused for a moment, then figured out what Mark was thinking. It might work, and if it did it would be a huge step toward cleaning up the city.

"We suspect that there are bigger fish out there. We just don't know who or where to find them," John started, "would you be willing to help us out?"

"What? Are you crazy? They'd kill me! I'd be dead by morning if I took an offer like that! Look, Mark, I said I'd be willing to quit the business if I could. If a better offer came along, but I'm not *dying* to make that change, you understand?"

"Joey, this is your opportunity to get out, start clean and do some good. Think of it as making amends for all the things you've been doing wrong. All you have to do is give up the names of the top tier bosses and then you are free. Kill the serpent by cutting off its head."

"No way. Didn't you hear me? They'd kill me. Matter of fact. It's not worth it."

"They can't kill a dead man, Joey," John retorted.

Joey's face blanched at the thought of John smothering him where he laid, but John's expression indicated there was more to his logic than base violence.

"What are you talking about?"

"If you were to have a complication here in the hospital, say, a blood clot," Mark added, "that resulted in your death, there would be no reason to hunt you down and kill you. The bosses would think that you gave them up before you died, we'd have the information to shut them down, and you could start a whole new life. Everyone wins. Well, almost everyone."

Joey sat for a minute considering the offer. He switched his attention to John.

"You can guarantee that?"

"If you can keep your mouth shut about who you were and what you did, we can set everything up. Once you commit, there is no turning back and keeping the secret is squarely on your shoulders. Understand?"

"Yeah. Yeah, I understand."

"That means that Joey Davis will be legally dead. You will get a new identity and a new life. You will have no contacts with anyone from your past. In exchange, you will agree to give us all the information you can in order to put these guys away. Are you sure you understand? This is a massive change for you."

"Can I sleep on it?"

"I wish you would, Joey. We'll be back tomorrow, OK?"

Joey looked at the pair as they stood to leave. Was this really happening? Had he really been given a second chance to live his life right? Was it worth the risk? Then a question suddenly popped in his head.

"Mark?"

"Yeah, Joey?"

"A minute ago, you said '*we'd* have the information.' Are you a cop now?"

"No."

"Then, what's your interest in all this?"

"I just think you need a second chance. That's why you're here."

Joey considered the statement with a look of confusion.

"How do you mean?"

Mark looked at John as if asking permission. John simply shrugged his shoulders in response. "If you trust him," he seemed to say.

Mark leaned in close to Joey and whispered, "I'm the one that shot you. Don't make me regret it."

Joey slumped back in the bed, speechless. A wave of emotion raced through him as he watched his friend and assailant walk out the door.

John pulled the door shut behind them and told the officer standing watch not to let anyone in or out except hospital staff. Phone access to the room had been restricted since admission, so there was no way for Joey to contact the outside world except through law enforcement. He would have no distractions to consider the offer in full. Mark and John both hoped he would make the right decision. Mark considered the options if he didn't.

Around 2:00 the following day John stopped by Mark's house. He knocked on the door and momentarily was greeted by Mark, his hair still wet from his shower.

"Hey, man. I'm almost ready. Come on in."

Thompson stepped inside and made himself at home.

"You want anything to drink? I'll be done in just a minute. I got a little side tracked after lunch."

"No problem. What do you have on tap?"

"Oh, a little of everything. Help yourself. You know where everything is."

John strode to the kitchen and browsed through the refrigerator, finally deciding on a Dr. Pepper. He popped the top on the icy can and returned to his seat in the living room. Mark emerged from the hallway, tucking his shirt tail in as he made his way to the living room as well.

"I figured you'd have a Mountain Dew. There's a whole case in there that nobody wants."

"Same here. I haven't had one since they added brominated vegetable oil to the mix. It just doesn't taste right anymore." John took a long sip from the can and stood up, "You ready?"

"Yep. Ready as I'll ever be. Have you heard from him?"

"Nope. I talked to the Chief about the plan. He's good with it except the means to pay for it. Setting someone up for a new life can be pricey."

"Yeah, I was thinking about that last night. I may have a solution there as well. I was also wondering what the next move would be if he turned the offer down."

Reduction

John opened the front door and turned to face Mark, "I know what you mean. I've been thinking about that too. You realize if he doesn't take the offer, your cover is blown, right?"

The thought slapped Mark in the face. He'd been worried about what would happen to Joey. He hadn't considered that Joey might flip the tables and make him a marked man.

"Oh, shit," was all he could say.

They arrived at the hospital just before 3:00 and made their way to the elevators. Arriving on the sixth floor they passed the nurse's station and hung a left down the corridor to Joey's room. A uniformed officer stood watch at the door, just like the evening before.

"I.D. please," he said as the duo approached. John showed his badge as Mark fumbled for his wallet.

"He's with me. Friend of the shooting victim," John said, "Anyone been in there with him?"

"The doctor stopped in about 45 minutes ago and the nurse has been in twice since I came on duty, sir."

"Good. We'll need some privacy. Can you see that we're not disturbed?"

"Will do."

Mark and John stepped through the doorway and into the darkened room. Joey was still sleeping off the morning pain medication and was slow to realize he had company. When he finally came to his senses he realized why they were there.

"Morning, boys," he muttered as he tried to stretch among all the hoses and wires.

"Afternoon, actually," John replied, "Sleep well, did we?"

"Thanks to the morphine drip."

Reduction

John managed a small laugh, "Did you think about our conversation at all?"

"Yeah. Yeah, I did," Joey said as he fumbled for the bed control. Finally getting a grip on the device he raised himself to a sitting position and reached for his water.

"And?"

"And...I don't really have much of a choice, do I? I mean, I take the offer and get out with a clean record and a new life. I don't and I have to do time. When I get out I still don't have anything to look forward to, plus I have a dirty record to boot.

"At the end of the day, it's kind of like Mark said. I got a second chance to do something right. If I pass it up, I might as well be face down and dead like the others that day."

Mark managed to smile a bit. He felt relieved that Joey had accepted the offer.

"I just wish you hadn't shot me to get the point across, you son of a bitch," Joey smiled, jabbing at his friend.

"Hey, now," Mark spat, "I tried to call you but you were too busy to talk. Remember?"

"Yeah, yeah, whatever. Anyway, I got the message," Joey got serious for just a second, "Thanks for caring. Seriously."

"I just hated to see you go that way. You're better than that."

"Ok, ladies," John started, "you two can make up later. Right now we need to get some information and get ready for you to die off, young man."

Joey seemed a little uncomfortable at the choice of words John had, but he knew what he meant. It was time to live up to his end of the deal and then 'pass away' quietly.

For the next couple of hours Joey unloaded the details of who he knew, who was in charge, shipping, receiving, distribution, and warehousing. Any aspect he could think of regarding the drug trade in the local area. John filled page after page of his small pocket notepad with names and locations, physical descriptions and schedules. Likewise, Mark had brought a small notepad and jotted down the details Joey laid before them. That way they stood a better chance of covering all the information and could cross reference if needed.

When he had exhausted all of his knowledge, Joey sat back in the bed and looked at the men, "That's all I've got, guys. So, how does this whole 'death' thing work?"

"Chief has a plan that will get you out of here. It's contingent on the validity of the information you just provided. We'll follow up, discreetly, on the leads and if everything looks legit we follow through with the next step."

Reduction

"That's what I mean, what's the next step? My info is solid. Some things might have changed since the shooting, but it won't have been much. Names won't have changed, and I doubt the locations will have...at least this soon."

"I'm just taking a guess here, I don't actually know what the plan is. I'd say that the hospital will fake your paperwork and list you as dead. The coroner will file the paperwork and issue a death certificate and you will then be legally declared dead. Meanwhile, you will be moved to another hospital to complete your recovery under your new identity. Once you are discharged you will be relocated to a new city, placed in a *legal* new occupation, and set on your way."

"What about testimony? Will I have to testify at trial against these guys?"

Reduction

"Well, I'm no legal expert, but I'd say it would be pretty hard to call a dead man to testify against anyone," Mark winked at his friend.

"Plus," John added nodding toward Mark, "If he does his job right, there won't be a trial to be had."

Joey just looked at his friend, still unsure what to make of him and his new job.

As investigators followed up on all of the information the Chief began making calls to arrange for the imminent demise of Joey Davis. When confirmation of that information began to roll in, Dahlgren decided it was time to call John in for some second opinions.

"Have a seat."

"Thank you, sir. What's on your mind?" John asked as he pulled a chair up at the Chief's desk.

"Things are checking out on the Davis case. I need to get the ball rolling on his new life. My problem isn't the paperwork side of things. It's the financial side."

"I understand. Specter and I were discussing that the other day. This situation is very, um, personal to him. He has advised me that he would be willing to waive his compensation for the job to help offset the cost to relocate Mr. Davis."

Dahlgren's eyebrows arced high on his face, "He's quite a crusader, this friend of yours, John. That would be a...substantial amount of money to walk away from. Does he realize that?"

"He doesn't know the exact dollar amount, but he is well aware that it is a lot of money. I think he would prefer not to know exactly how much. Still, he insists that Davis' second chance is more important. If giving up the cash takes the burden off of his witness protection arrangements he is willing to do it."

Reduction

Dahlgren chuckled. "I'm impressed. It amazes me that a man with such esteem for doing charitable deeds can deal such devastation. Sometimes I think I would like to meet this guy."

"Who knows," Thompson smiled, "maybe you already have."

It took two days to verify the data Joey had provided, but for the most part he was spot on. Dahlgren made a series of calls to put everything in motion. Soon the paperwork had been doctored and it was time to doctor Joey.

Just after two in the afternoon the doctor came in and shot a drug into Joey's IV. He leaned over and almost whispered into his ear, "When you wake up, you'll feel like a new man." With that, he smiled and closed the door behind him as he left. A couple of minutes later and the effects were beginning to show as Davis' heart rate began to slow and a deep drowsy feeling washed over him.

"Code blue 612. Code blue 612." The call repeated over the PA system. A trio of nurses broke from the nearby station and hurried down the hallway to the room. Almost simultaneously, the doctor reached the doorway and bolted in past the guard.

"Crash cart! Now!"

The nurse nearest the door rushed out and quickly returned with a small cart full of medical supplies. The guard stepped aside with a shocked look on his face and tried to peek in as she raced by. Not sure what was going on he reached for his cell phone and called the precinct.

Amid the shouting in the room, nurses and other staff streamed in and out at an incredible pace. The guard could hear the heart monitor flatline followed by repeated shouts and the clanging of instruments. Finally there was silence. Staff members began to slowly exit the room one at a time. As the doorway opened he heard, "Time of death, three thirty-seven."

A few minutes later Thompson and Dahlgren stepped off the elevator and approached the officer.

"What happened?"

"Not sure sir. Everything has been fine until about an hour ago. The nurse went in to check on him and yelled out 'code blue.' The next thing I know there was a half-dozen people running in and out of the room. I heard the monitor go flat and they worked on him a while longer. The doctor pronounced him just before you got out of the elevator."

Dahlgren looked at John and sighed.

"I guess that ends your guard duty here. I'll expect a full report in the morning. Go home, son."

"Thank you, sir. I'll have it for you first thing."

Reduction

The doctor was soon back at the door and led the pair inside to discuss the events. As he finished up, Dahlgren shook his hand and thanked him for his help.

"The boys from the morgue should be here to collect him in a bit. I've seen to it that all the paperwork has been taken care of."

"We'll have a car pick up the body in a while. Again, thanks for all your help."

"No problem. Have a nice day, gentlemen."

As the doctor left the room, Dahlgren made one final call.

"Pick up in one hour. Don't be late. You know the final destination? That's right. Everything has been arranged. Yes. That's the name. Contact me after completion, please."

He ended the call and returned the phone to its case. Looking across the room to the bed he couldn't help but notice the condition of the place.

Reduction

The contents of the crash cart lay scattered across the bed and floor and equipment of various types crowded the bed on two sides. Among it all was Joey, silent and still. His chest didn't rise and fall, nor did his eyes flutter.

"He's gonna have one hell of a headache in a couple of days," Dahlgren muttered.

"Mark?"

"Yeah, honey?"

"Have you seen today's paper?"

Mark turned to face Angie, curious about the tone in her voice.

"No, why?"

"It says here that Joey Davis died yesterday. Have you heard anything?"

Mark sat there, unsure of what to say. Of course he knew. He knew more about it than she did, but he hadn't considered the obituary in the paper.

More to the point, he hadn't considered the possibility of Angie reading the obituary page.

"Uh, what? What does it say?"

"It says here that Joey died yesterday at Saint Matthew Hospital after complications from a gunshot wound. He had no surviving family and that the funeral arrangements will be handled by the state. How did he get shot? He wasn't a hunter, was he?"

"No, not that I can recall. Are you sure it was him? I mean he can't have been the only Joey Davis around."

"I guess it could be someone else. There's no picture and the address listed isn't in the area I remember you said he lived."

"Tell you what," Mark started, trying to put his wife at ease, "I'll see if I can find out anything tomorrow. I'll try to get hold of some of the guys from work and see if they can confirm anything."

Reduction

Angie nodded her head in agreement. She didn't seem to be in shock at the possible revelation, but surprised. After all, Joey and Mark were friends, but it had been a while since they had heard anything from him, let alone actually seen him. Angie seemed to be satisfied with Mark's offer to follow up and find out more. Mark was relieved that he had managed to avoid the situation for the rest of the evening.

The following morning Mark called John for advice on handling the situation. John's reply was simple and direct.

"Tell her what happened."

"What?"

"Tell her what happened. Davis got tied up in drugs and gangs and as a result he was caught in the crossfire of an intense gang war. As for burial arrangements, there will be no funeral for him since he had no family here that we can locate, so his body has been transferred to the closest next of kin we could find."

"Who would that be? I know she's going to ask."

"OK, then tell her he was sent to the body farm. That ought to settle it."

Mark thought about the idea for a moment.

"She won't like it."

"Nobody's asking her to," The tone of John's voice became more sympathetic, "Look, I know you don't like lying to your wife, Mark, but this is one time where a man's life is on the line. I would think that if she knew the extent of what's been going on she would understand the importance of being lied to. Then again, if she knew the facts as a whole, she'd probably kill you and me. I'd rather avoid the whole situation, personally."

"Yeah. You're right. I was just hoping to avoid having to explain any of it, let alone having to lie about it."

Later that evening, as he sat at the kitchen table working on a cold glass of sweet tea, Angie strolled into the room and pulled up the seat beside his. He knew what was coming.

"Honey," she began, leaning in to get his full attention, "did you get a chance to talk to anyone today about Joey?"

"Hmm?" Mark stalled with the hopes to avoid the conversation before it started, but Angie would have none of it.

"Honey, did you find out anything about Joey today?"

"Oh, yeah. Um, I spoke to John today. He said that either one of two things happened."

"And...?"

"And, in either case there was no formal funeral here."

"Well, what happened? Where is he buried? Who do we need to send flowers to? Come on, Mark, you're being very aloof here."

"Aloof? That's a word you don't hear everyday. Where'd you pull that from?"

"Don't question my vocabulary, young man," she smiled, "now, tell me what you found out."

"You won't like it."

"Which one?"

"Either."

Angie could tell that Mark didn't want to discuss the issue, but she couldn't understand why.

"Come on, tell me. I won't get upset."

Mark turned and looked at her for a minute, then glanced back at his glass.

"John says that since they couldn't find any close family connections here they would have either sent the body to the nearest relatives, which would probably be out of state. Or," he hesitated, almost as if bracing for impact, "he could have been sent to the body farm, where they send unclaimed bodies."

Angie's face flushed, "I know what the body farm is. I can't believe they'd do that. How could they do that?"

Mark considered options quickly and blurted out, "John said that they most likely sent the body to the nearest kin. He wasn't sure and I don't know who it would have been."

Angie stared at him blankly for a moment and opened her mouth as if to say something before reconsidering.

"Ask him to find out. I would like to send some flowers *somewhere*."

Acting on John's advice they devised a plan to send flowers to a retirement home. Mark would make the arrangements and John would make sure that a "Thank You" card was sent for closure. By the end of the week everything was decided and flowers were soon on their way.

With Joey's demise finally out of the way it was back to work. John had considered sending Mark on hits for some of the bigger targets right away, but the chief had decided to let things play out for a while and cement the notion that no information had been leaked to law enforcement. They would monitor from a distance and see what, if anything, changed. So, Mark was offered some "light work" as John called it.

His next job focused on a slimy little fellow that had been working local gun shows and trading straw purchased firearms for cash. His typical M.O. was to linger outside the gun show entrances and exits and watch for an unsuspecting attendee with a firearm of interest. After all, why pay to get in when you can do business in the free parking lot? He would approach the individual and ask if he was selling. If so, he would ask the price and play the gullible buyer role to a T. Payment would always be made in cash and outside the view of the ATF agents that always attended these events undercover. They were there to catch people like him, but they were stretched so thin due to sequestrations and budget cuts that the manpower couldn't be spared. Signs were posted around asking patrons not to participate in sales outside of the show, but, as Mark knew, money speaks louder than morals in many cases and criminals who are determined to commit a crime are going to regardless of rules. That's what makes them criminals.

John described him as having "carnie-like rat face features" and he would be easy to spot. When Mark opened the rather thin file on him he couldn't help but laugh. The single photograph was exactly as John described. Short stature at only five foot five with a round little face, narrow, deep set eyes and a sharply pointed nose, his image screamed "rodent."

He had a surprisingly small rap sheet with mostly minor arrests. There wasn't a single felony in the package. Nothing that would have made his direct purchase of firearms illegal to begin with. This guy didn't want his name on the paper trail to anything he sold to the gangsters.

Mark began to think about the target and consider his crimes. Was he worthy of reduction? After all, he had multiple straw purchases that resulted in weapon sales to drug dealers and their thugs. Those weapons were used against law enforcement and civilians alike all the time, but was it worse than the Fast and Furious project undertaken by the federal government just a few years earlier? None of the ATF or DOJ officials involved in that disaster were sentenced to die for their actions even though the end results were the same. Perhaps it would be best to set the guy up in a sting and bust him on the felonies he was committing. As simple as pulling the trigger on this one would be, Mark was having a difficult time making the decision to accept the job. Maybe it was because everyone else had a lengthy wrap sheet. He could *see* their evil doings and justify the move. This one was different. He closed the folder and set it aside. Perhaps John could enlighten him a bit more and give him more to work with to make the call.

He met John the next day and expressed his concerns about the job.

"I understand. I actually wondered if this would strike you differently since the guy appears to be so clean. Trust me. He's dirty. He just hides it well."

"Yeah, I noticed that. Have you considered setting up a sting operation on him and busting him that way? Maybe he could be more valuable as an informant."

"We have, but we'd have to catch him in the act of a sale to make it stick. I would love to catch him in the act of modding some of the weapons if possible, but that is a long shot."

"Modding? How so?"

"Well," John started, "in some recent busts we've made there have been some rifles that were modified to be select fire capable. This is a major NFA violation. We can't prove it was this guy, but we suspect it's him. He's pretty sharp and knows his weapons. We feel like he's fully capable of making the modifications, we just can't connect the dots."

Mark studied the case again, considering alternatives and complications.

"Still," he replied, "I don't know. He looks the part of a weasel, and what your telling me is that this guy is more of a felon than some of the people

I've already taken out, but there's no supporting evidence. That's my problem. I can't pull the trigger on him with a clean conscience because I have only speculation and conjecture. There's no trail, you see?"

"I got you. No problem. I tell you what, I'll talk to the chief and see if I can get him to work up a sting. Sit on the info and I'll see what he says. I have another job waiting for you if you want to take a look at it."

"Sure thing. Did you bring it with you?"

"No, I left it at the office. Again, it's not a big one, and it's not tied to the info from Joey, but it is a situation that needs to be dealt with."

"OK, just let me know and I'll take a look."

"Sounds good. I'll try to get something to you tomorrow morning. That OK with you?"

"That will work. Meanwhile I may do a little research on Mr. Rat Face here myself."

Reduction

The rest of the day Mark casually checked out the weapons dealer, looking up his address on the city maps and checking out the neighborhood. As he drove down the street leading in front of the man's house he was surprised at the quality of the surroundings. It was an older part of town, probably developed during the fifties or early sixties, but it still retained a certain nostalgic charm. The yards were all well manicured and clean of clutter. Most vehicles were recent models with a couple of classic muscle cars under cover in a driveway here or there. It wasn't the picture he had in mind for a man of this caliber to be living in; not high society, but then not the ghetto either.

Mark still hoped that a sting could be arranged. He disliked the idea of taking a shot in this area. Besides the logistical difficulty of getting in and out, there were no good vantage points for a hide. On top of it all, the thought of shooting someone in this neighborhood made him shudder at the social trauma he would unleash. After all, people here had kids. It was a family location, not one for an assassination.

Then it dawned on him, he never looked at the man's marital status. Was he married? Did he have children? That had never crossed his mind before. Just what he needed, more complications to consider. Was he beginning to get soft? Could he continue to do this kind of work? Mark decided it would be best to stop for the day and go home. No more would he worry about work today. That would come tomorrow.

Mark woke early the next morning and made his way to the kitchen for a cup of coffee. Digging through the cabinets he could find nothing that interested him for breakfast so he settled for one of the kids toaster pastries and resigned himself to a seat on the deck. The air was cool but fresh and helped him to clear his mind and focus on what he had to do that day.

John would no doubt be calling him within a few hours to brief him on the other job. He would want to meet and cover the details, which might provide him an opportunity to follow up on the rat faced man a bit more. Perhaps an opportunity to find out where he went to make his illicit weapon deals. Somewhere that could afford better hide opportunities and a more "appropriate" setting for the task at hand.

He sat in silence as the sun crested the horizon and bathed the countryside in a brilliant yellow orange hue. Lost in thought and engrossed by the tranquility about him he didn't even realize that Angie had slipped onto the deck with her own mug of coffee and a fresh blueberry muffin.

"Good morning, sunshine," she said quietly as she pulled a chair up beside him, "Come here often?"

"Hey, babe. I didn't know you were up yet."

"Yeah, I noticed that. You must be worn out the way you tossed and turned and carried on all night. I don't know what had you so upset, but you kept me awake half the night."

Mark didn't realize he had been that bad. He knew he had slept poorly, but he had slept. He couldn't recall any particularly bad dreams, but then his recollection was scattered nonsense, so he wasn't sure what kept him in such turmoil through the night.

"Sorry. I knew I was restless, I didn't realize it was that bad."

"That's OK. I know you're still under a lot of pressure trying to find stable work and all. Besides, if you could put up with me during pregnancy with both kids, I can tolerate the occasional rough night of yours. There's just one thing that bothers me," she took a long sip of her coffee as she let the comment hang.

"What's that?"

Reduction

"Well, if you insist on talking in your sleep, I wish you would make some sense out of it. I couldn't understand a thing you said last night," Angie smiled at Mark sheepishly, prodding him for a response.

Mark wasn't sure what to say, now he really wished he could recall what had been on his mind. What if he had talked about a job he had done? What if he had mentioned a name or location? His relaxing time on the deck was quickly fading into a worrisome situation that he had hoped to avoid.

"Huh? I talked in my sleep? What did I say?"

Angie snickered, "That's just it, most of what I heard was complete gibberish; mumbling. Oh there were a few words once or twice, but they didn't make any sense, although I think you were dreaming about killing mice or rats or something once. It was very frustrating."

She sat back in her chair and finished off her muffin and coffee before announcing that she had to get ready for work. Rising from her seat she leaned to give Mark a quick kiss on his furrowed forehead before returning to the kitchen.

"Holy crap," was all Mark could think. He wasn't one to talk in his sleep very often. As he recalled that was probably only the second or third time in their marriage that he had done it at all. Each prior episode was during very stressful times as well and had been early in their marriage when they were tight on budget and jobs were new. He was going to have to deal with this quickly to make sure it didn't get out of hand.

As expected John's call came just before lunch and they met at one of the usual designated diners for a quick break down of the data. After the briefing and a quick burger John brought up a second topic for Mark's consideration.

"I spoke to the chief this morning about your concerns with our rat faced carnie friend."

"And? What's his opinion?"

"Well, he is in agreement with you to an extent. If the man could be caught in the act he might be a valuable source of information. Then again, he may be more trouble than he's worth. Either way, an arrest would have to take place while he is in the act, which could be a bad place to be. We don't have anyone we can slip in to set him up either. The only way we can get him in the act is if someone tails him and calls us when it happens and we can have a rapid response team in the area. That's not an easy thing to coordinate, but it could be done…with reliable intel."

"Which you don't have."

"Which we don't have," John nodded in agreement.

"So, what's the final word then?"

"Chief is willing to arrange a sting if you are willing to provide the intel. He wants you to be the 'reliable' part and even mentioned you providing overwatch during the sting, just in case things go badly."

"Hmm. He's a trusting soul. Does he have any idea who I am?"

"No. But since the incident with Joey and your response to the financial demands of setting him up with a new life, well, you've impressed him. You've been careful in every operation and have caused no collateral damage other than some burnt vehicles and noise pollution. He knows that I trust you and he knows that he can trust me. All things being equal, he trusts you based on what he *does* know."

Mark thought about it as he nursed the last of his soft drink. Finally he looked John in the face,

Reduction

"Why me for overwatch? The department has snipers. Shouldn't they be on task for that job?"

"The department does have snipers. Good men too. Good shots and well disciplined. The chief will likely have one or two of them around, but since it will likely be you making the call for us to roll in, he would like you there as an added level of backup. Understand this: your ONLY target will be Rat Face. Nobody else. If we roll up and start taking fire you are to drop him and leave immediately."

"I don't know man. I don't like it. It's too close. Too many people involved. Too much opportunity for my cover to be blown. On top of that I have no idea where this guy does his business at. He might be dealing in a Wal-Mart parking lot for all I know. How am I supposed to drop a guy in a public place like that?"

John sat quietly for a moment. Mark's concerns were all valid points. He knew that Mark wouldn't have said anything if they weren't or if more options were available. All he could do was agree and ask, "What do you want me to tell the chief?"

Mark sat for a minute. What did he want to say? If the guy was as low as he was supposed to be he needed to be taken down, but with the potential for something to go wrong being so high, he didn't want to be taken down at the same time.

"Tell him I will act as his eyes, but being a trigger man on this one will depend on the situation at the moment. I won't pull a trigger unless I feel like it needs to be done. Depending on where it happens, I may not even have a weapon on me."

John shot Mark a look of sarcastic disbelief, "Seriously? Who are you talking to?"

Mark smiled, "I said 'may not.' OK?"

Both men smiled at the notion and then decided it was time to part company for the day. Mark had two jobs to follow up on and he needed to get back to his shop to begin that planning process. Once he was home he only had a little time before the family would demand his attention so he focused on the second case. He had grown tired of the rat-faced man and wanted to see something different, something he could do with a clear conscience.

The second case reminded him quite a lot of his first hit. The area frequented by the suspect wasn't too far away, in fact, from the very location of that first assignment. This was a small time pusher as well, but he was gaining quite a reputation at strong-arm tactics and violence. He was recently sought as the prime suspect in a poorly executed drive-by, but was later cleared when no witnesses could, or would, identify him. It always struck Mark as odd that the people that were often the victims of crime, even violent crime, would scream for justice to be done only to wash their hands of involvement when it came to prosecuting the criminals themselves. "We want justice," they seemed to shout, "but we don't want to be involved in it." And so bad people walked the streets. So people like Mark could do the job that police couldn't. Odd indeed.

He finally decided on a point to start his reconnaissance for the 27 year old man. This fellow, like many others in the area, was into cars. He liked to show off his flashy rims and gold accents with the rest of his peers at a local dive not far from his only known address. Home addresses were typically unreliable starting points because, as most of these people knew, it would be the first place the police would look for them. They rarely ever lived at a listed address and, in fact, some addresses didn't even exist at all. It was usually better to learn where they hung out and pick up a trail from there. Not necessarily easier, but better.

Mark studied the case until he heard the back door then hurriedly put things away.

Chapter 7

It was a beautiful day in the downtown area. The sky was a brilliant blue without a cloud to be seen and, despite the roar of traffic on the busy streets, Mark could still make out the sounds of birds in the trees and bushes about the neighborhood. He turned his truck down a secondary street and then over a few blocks to a parking garage where he slipped up to the roof level and found a spot on the southeast corner overlooking his target neighborhood.

It wasn't quite 10:00 yet, so foot traffic in the area was still minimal as he stared through his compact binoculars down the streets in the distance. Mark always thought it was funny how people put so much more emphasis on outward appearances than they did on personal improvement. Each house looked to be a build from the 1930s, probably a WPA project, and had definitely seen better days. Most had some degree of clutter in the yards while barbed wire and block walls to keep undesirables out, on both sides of the law, were commonplace. The place had a typical run-down appearance that you would expect a strong criminal presence to thrive in. Yet, all along the street sat cars with rims that cost thousands and custom paint jobs that cost thousands more. Each, no doubt, had a massive sound system that was probably worth more than the car itself. And then you consider that with all the investment into these cars, their trade in value was non-existent. Nobody would ever pay what had been invested in them. It was like flushing money down the drain for social appearances. The irony was that Mark was sitting in his beater of a pickup casting judgment on the decisions of others to drive a car tailored to their desires.

Thanks to his money management since this new line of work opened he could easily have bought a newer truck, but this one was paid for and still ran fine. He mused at the thought of him in a pimped out truck for a moment before a flash of sunlight caught his attention.

Peering through the glasses again he spotted the hangout where his quarry was most likely to be found. One of the area punks had rolled up in his car with the chrome tall walker rims and now sat in front of the old gas station on the corner apparently waiting for someone. With the glare across the windshield and the distance between them he couldn't identify the driver, but he could tell he wasn't alone in the car and wasn't getting out. Mark decided to improve his options and flipped the center seat console down, then open to reveal his latest toy: a pair of Zeiss 10 x 50mm binoculars.

Raising the lenses to his eyes the field of view became crisp and clear with amazing detail. He could easily see the paint job on the vehicle sporting a candy bar wrapper design with a derogatory variant of the brand name in full bold colors. Though still distant, Himes could tell with the larger glasses that neither occupant was his mark for the day. He would have to wait a while longer.

Finally, after sitting in the cab of his truck for most of the morning a second and then third car joined the first at the curb. He swung the glasses up again and watched as two females stepped out of one vehicle. He estimated them to be in their early twenties with dyed hair and numerous piercings. Tattoos could clearly be seen from wrist to shoulder on both girls as well as around their legs and ankles. Himes' first thought was that they looked like something from a bad rap video.

"Eye of the beholder, I guess." He muttered quietly to himself.

From the third car emerged another girl and two males. It was difficult to see their faces at first since their caps were in the way, but soon he got a fair enough glimpse at each to know that they weren't who he was looking for either. Himes' frustration was beginning to mount. He was tired of wasting a gorgeous day watching for this guy to establish some kind of routine.

He decided to give it one more hour and then he was going to break camp and follow other efforts. After all, he still had his weapons dealer to consider. Reaching over into his lunch box he produced the thermos of tea he packed earlier that morning and took a long satisfying sip. He considered the monotony of what it must be like on a stakeout. He could never comprehend the boredom of waiting and watching the same house for days trying to catch someone. Of course, that was the way it was always done in the movies, and as he had learned first hand what you see in the movies doesn't always happen in the real world.

Reduction

Ten minutes before he had decided to pack up and go another vehicle approached the first three. Even from this distance Mark could swear he heard the thump of the sound system as the doors opened and his man stepped out. Mark made mental notes about the car, driver and direction it had arrived from and fumbled for his notepad while trying not to take his eyes from the scene. As he scratched out details into his pad he watched the girls approach and began hanging on the newcomers. Being as far away as he was, he couldn't be positive, but was pretty confident in the assumption that at least one was smoking a less than legal cigarette and they were all in various stages of inebriation.

He continued to observe for a few minutes before he noticed a new vehicle approaching the assembly. Figuring it was more of the entourage arriving he let his attention slip. Then he heard the gunfire.

Reduction

The car approached from a slow start a couple of blocks away, giving the occupants time to ready their weapons. As they neared the group of men and women the windows rolled all the way down and the barrels of a half-dozen various weapons protruded through the openings. As the car approached 75 feet the triggers were pulled and lead sprayed the bystanders, guilty and not-so guilty alike.

Mark's man wasn't the first hit, but was definitely down. He fell among the tangled limbs of one of the girls and his passenger. Himes could see movement among the bodies as the car accelerated away from the scene and turned the corner. He scanned back and forth across the bodies on the sidewalk. One of the girls was fumbling for her cell phone as blood streamed down her forearm and dripped from her elbow. One of the males sat upright against the building with a large red patch of blood spreading across his upper chest while another lay motionless in a growing pool of his own. Beside him lay another of the females, also motionless.

"Well, shit," was all Mark could muster. He grabbed his burn phone and quickly sent a message to John.

Reduction complete. I have competition. Call ASAP

About an hour later, Mark was on the phone with Thompson giving the details of the incident as he observed them through the binoculars. John was a bit surprised at the details he was able to recount over the distance he watched.

"I think I'll add a pair of those binoculars to my Christmas list this year," he remarked with a snort.

"They cost about a half a low-life drug dealer a pair," Mark quipped without missing a beat.

Mark continued the debriefing with a detailed description of the vehicle and what he could tell of the occupants, which wasn't much. The shooting started while he was distracted and by the time he had the glasses to his eyes the vehicle was on the way out of the area. He was able to make reasonable guesses at the types of weapons used, but from the distance he couldn't be positive. Even the number of muzzles protruding was no more than a guess.

"Well, that's more than we would have had, Mark. I appreciate the input. Did you want to see if the chief will honor this as a job for you?"

"No. All I did was observe. I didn't have a weapon on hand to do the job with even if I had the opportunity."

John smiled, "You want us to track the shooters down and cut the check to them?"

"Yeah, you do that. I'll bet that would be the toughest delivery in history." Mark smiled at the thought.

"So, have you come up with anything on our weapons dealer yet?"

"Nothing solid. Any word on a sting?"

Reduction

"It's coming together. We just need a location and a time frame."

"Alright. I'll get back on him and see if I can figure some sort of routine. He's a hard target to put a schedule on, you know?"

"I understand. Do what you can. I'm trying to turn rocks on my end as well. Maybe we can work something up soon."

Mark returned to his folder on the rat-faced weapon supplier and strained to find a pattern to the man's regimen. Finally, he had a revelation. The only guaranteed location he knew of to find the man was at the gun shows. He quickly brought up the schedule for upcoming shows and decided to attend. Besides, he might find something useful for his new trade and be able to kill two birds with one stone...so to speak.

The next show would be at the local expo center in three weeks. Mark wondered if that was too far away, but decided that it would have to be adequate. The plan would be as simple as he could make it. Go to the show, find his man and watch him deal in the parking lot. At the end of the day, follow him out and see where he took his purchases. Simple. That should give him a stakeout location and possibly a dealing location.

Like most of the United States, Mark's hometown was integral to the gun culture since before the establishment of the city itself. Firearms had always been there and, despite the best efforts of many in the political arenas, seemed as if they were always would be. Crowds at the gun shows were usually respectable.

The date finally rolled around for the show and Mark made his way across town to the expo center. As he suspected, the parking lot was pretty full. Recent talk of legislation on numerous levels had prompted a buying panic once again. Not as big this time as it had been around the 2012 election, but still, some items were becoming difficult to find. Almost as difficult to find as a decent parking place.

He finally started across the asphalt towards the main building where a considerable line stood with a wide array of firearms for sale or trade. He scanned the crowd and across the parking lot with no sign of his man to be found. Time to go inside.

After several minutes Mark finally got in the building and began his shopping with a clockwise survey of the numerous tables. Among the many varieties of long guns and sidearms were scattered tables of parts, ammunition and reloading components, and what seemed to be truck loads of surplus gear from all different branches of the military from all over the world. Mark stopped at one of these tables to inspect a Kevlar vest. He'd never actually picked one up before and was surprised at the weight of it.

"Man, that had to be one hot suit to wear in Iraq," he muttered to himself.

"Sure was," a voice replied over his shoulder, "But after the sun went down it wasn't so bad. Deserts get a lot colder than you'd think. Nothin' there to hold the heat in."

Mark smiled at the man and simply said, "Well, I thank you for your service, sir. Glad you're not over there anymore."

The man casually nodded back with a light smile and made his way farther down the aisle. Mark continued in the opposite direction taking note of the array of wares at each turn until he saw something familiar down an adjacent aisle. He wasn't sure, but he thought he saw the man he was after. Through the crowd he stared trying to locate the individual with no luck. Quickly he worked his way around to where he thought the man had been.

Reduction

He noticed that on the table were a large selection of AK's, AR's, M1A's, and semi-auto pistols patterned after sub-machine guns and PDW's, or Personal Defense Weapons. He suspected that the selection of weapons fit the profile of products that the man specialized in, but he knew he wouldn't dare do the paperwork himself for a purchase. Perhaps he had seen someone else buy something and was now following them to the parking lot to work a straw purchase. Mark's eyes quickly turned to the closest entrance. There he was. The rat-faced fellow was heading out the door.

Mark hurried through the crowd as quickly as he could and slipped outside. The sudden change in ambient light made him squint as his eyes adjusted and he panned the parking lot. Rat Face was heading down the first row of cars at a quick pace. Mark would have a difficult time catching him without looking suspicious himself. He quickened his own pace and headed toward the same row. Almost halfway down the row the Rat Face turned between a couple of cars and moved to the second row, then across the aisle to the third. Mark moved to a van and watched the man as he walked to an older model cargo minivan. The vehicle suited him, and his occupation, well. From his position Mark could see the man relatively clearly as he opened the driver's side door and reached inside. A second later he was sitting in the van. Mark considered getting his truck in case the man left so he could follow. He looked to where his truck was then back at the man's van just as a pair of young men walked by the man's front bumper.

Rat Face stepped out and approached the pair, apparently inquiring about the rifles they had slung over their shoulders. They talked for a few moments before the first young man handed Rat Face his rifle. An AK-74, by the looks of it, Mark thought. After fondling the firearm for a few minutes he handed it back and received the second rifle. It was an AR-15 to be sure. A few minutes passed as the trio talked. Rat Face dug into his pocket and produced a large roll of cash and swiftly peeled off a number of bills and handed them to the first man then did the same to the second, much to his delight. The two young men quickly returned to the show with cash in hand and smiles on their faces. Rat Face looked around quickly before opening the van and quickly putting the new acquisitions inside. Mark couldn't be sure, but thought he saw additional weapons on the wall of the cargo compartment. With a smug smile he closed the van door and locked it, then scanned the parking lot for potential purchases and headed back toward the show entrance.

Mark thought for a minute on what his next move should be and decided that he would move his truck closer to the man's vehicle. Lunch was coming on fast and he knew that many patrons would be leaving to eat somewhere besides the concession stand inside. He didn't much blame anyone for that since the selection was pretty limited and the quality of food was not very good.

He started the engine on his truck and began his drive across the parking lot. Nothing was available on the first couple of rows. As he turned to go down the third row he noticed a car backing out a little more than two-thirds of the way down. The spot would be relatively close to Rat Face's van so Mark headed for it hoping no one else got it first. Almost out of instinct he glanced toward where the van was just in time to see the driver's side door close and the brake lights glow. Apparently Rat Face had finished shopping for the day. Either that or someone was stealing his truck. In either case, Mark needed to follow that vehicle.

Reduction

He quickly passed the parking spot and stopped at the end of the aisle. To his luck, Rat Face pulled out right in front of him and pulled through the gate of the parking lot, then turned right. Mark followed as quickly and closely as he could without trying to draw attention to himself. The vehicles trailed across town, away from the direction of Rat Face's house, for several miles until within sight of a large self storage facility.

Mark slowed down and pulled into the lot of a gas station across the street trying to position himself for a good vantage while out of sight enough not to be noticed. From his location he could see the van pass through the gates and pass the office, then turn down the second aisle and slowly drive to the end of the row of small garage doors where it came to a stop three doors from the end.

Rifling through his truck Mark finally produced his binoculars and dialed the focus in on the van. Rat Face appeared from inside the storage building and reached deep inside the van, extracting a pair of rifles. Immediately Mark recognized them as the pair that he had bought earlier. The man quickly stepped inside and tucked them away only to return and remove another pair from the vehicle. A second AR and a strange looking rifle Mark wasn't familiar with. It was a bullpup configuration, he knew, but the exact make and model were unknown to him. Again, he slipped inside and returned to the van a moment later only to produce a third pair of firearms.

An AK and an SKS with a folding stock. The SKS looked to have been modified to take a larger, possibly detachable, magazine, but in the brief moment he had to look at it he couldn't be sure. It occurred to Mark that he may very well have stashed a couple more firearms inside while he had been fumbling for his optics. The man stayed inside a bit longer this trip than before, but eventually returned to the van where he removed a box, apparently of some considerable weight by the look on his face.

As Rat Face disappeared into the structure once again Mark made note of the storage company and address as well as the specific unit that was being used. Mark pulled his burn phone from his jacket pocket and composed a simple text.

Found the toy store. Following delivery man to next stop. Please advise soonest.

Mark returned the phone to its place and swung the binoculars back up. His target was now loading boxes into the van. Mark suspected these to contain receivers or weapons broken down into smaller components for modification. John had mentioned that the man was also suspected of modifying some firearms into illegal automatic weapons and AOWs. Any Other Weapons, as the BATFE defined them.

The man quickly returned to the building and pulled the door down, locked it, and then scurried to the van's driver's side door. Mark stowed the field glasses and watched the van exit the facility. He turned left as Mark started the engine on his truck and prepared to follow suit.

Himes eased his vehicle to the edge of the pavement, being sure to give Rat Face a considerable lead so as not to draw attention to himself by following too closely. Mark finally pulled out into the rather light traffic and tried to blend in. He worried that he would be easily spotted since there were so few cars on the road, but continued on anyway. After several blocks the van slowed and turned right into another residential area. Mark slowed down as well and watched carefully as he approached the intersection. He saw the van parked on the side of the street just down from the intersection and decided to break of his pursuit. He continued past the street, but made a quick mental note of where the van was in relation to the road.

Could this second house be his workshop? Was he meeting a client?

Mark's phone rang, startling him. It was a message from John. He quickly found a place to pull over and checked his phone.

Do not engage. Note location. Go home. Will contact soonest.

Mark returned the phone into his pocket and tried to decide if there were any additional details he needed to pass on. Unable to remember any additional information, he put the truck in gear and pulled back out into traffic. Soon he was on his way to familiar territory and it wouldn't be long before he was back home.

Something was bothering him. The neighborhood that Rat Face lived in was all wrong. Mark fully expected to be in a lower-class neighborhood but instead found himself watching the van enter an older, but still rather nice, subdivision. Despite his best efforts, Mark could not recall any details of the man concerning a job or a family. Surely this could not be his only source of income. In addition, the house seemed to be a little large for just one man living alone. Mark decided to look back into the man's paperwork when he returned home.

He wondered what the legal ramifications would be for the two young men who sold Rat Face their firearms. If they were purchased legally they would likely be registered in the young men's names. Of course, Rat Face probably counted on this since it would help keep his clients anonymity secure. If those weapons were ever confiscated as part of a raid, the registration could be directly traced back to the original owners, who had never reported them stolen or would go to the trouble of changing the registration. "Oh well," Mark thought, "not my problem."

Mark pulled into his driveway and quickly went to his shop. He retrieved the file on Rat Face and verified the address. He decided to try a different approach to his research. A friend of his was a realtor and had informed him of a website that would show property ownership from state records. Perhaps he could verify the man's marital status based on property records. So, with that in mind, he opened the website and keyed in the address. Soon data filled the screen with assessed value, acreage, tax rate, and information about the owners. There, in the corner, were the names he'd been looking for. Albert and Marjorie Deason.

"Albert? Really?" Mark mused to himself, "He looks more like a rat than an 'Albert' to me."

Reduction

Mark quickly realized that Rat Face's dossier didn't have his last name as Deason. He double checked the paperwork to be sure. On the first page, just beside his picture, was the name Bradley Johnson. "Hmmm," Mark thought," He never struck me as a 'Bradley' either. Must come from a broken home. Mom probably remarried or something picking up a new surname in the process. Still, whose house is it?"

He logged onto the local courthouse website to see if he could find any information there that might shed some more light on the man's identity. After considerable digging he was able to find a marriage license for the Deasons dated March 26, 1987. A little more digging revealed that Marjorie had, indeed, been married before to a Robert Johnson in 1967 and subsequently divorced in the early 80's. Skipping ahead he found a marriage license for Bradley from 2011 when he married a girl named Mikaela Kinney. He found no certificate of divorce on the web archives, but there was a notice on the site that they were incomplete, but under construction. He knew that the volume of records had been undergoing digitization for some time and was surprised at how much was actually available. Still, the lack of a divorce record probably meant that he was still married. That could mean kids. Mark hoped the man wasn't stupid enough to demand his own execution.

Angie and the kids burst in the door as if they had won the lottery or something. The sudden commotion nearly scared Mark to death. He turned to see Andy, the 5-year-old, grinning from ear to ear. In his hand he held a small red square like a hard earned trophy.

"Look, Daddy! We gotted a movie!"

"Well, come over here and let's see what the entertainment for tonight is!"

Reduction

The youngster rushed to his father's chair and happily displayed the cover of the disc which revealed it to be the latest Pixar film. It had been in theaters when Mark's job search was just beginning and they couldn't afford to spend the money on dinner and a movie like they had every week for their "family nights."

Mark smiled at his son and said, "Alright, dude, we'll watch it after supper. OK?"

Andy smiled and placed the Blu Ray beside the player in the entertainment center before rushing to find his sister. Mark sat back in the chair once more, the smile across his face only thinly hiding his elation that they would be having a relaxing evening together at home, away from all the stress and frustration he had recently been under. That and the fact that, from time to time, he had to admit he liked a good Pixar movie himself.

Chapter 8

Saturday morning found Mark once again in the woods. Deer season had passed, but there were other things to hunt besides deer. On this morning he spent his time scouting for turkey. Though Mark didn't own many acres, it joined his parents land and that of several close friends and neighbors, so his available area to hunt was actually quite large. As he crossed the properties, checking trail cameras and watching for any signs of wildlife, his mind wandered back to the job he hadn't finished and the information that Joey had fed them during his recovery and relocation.

In his mind Mark began to piece the information together. He recalled that Joey had mentioned a larger figure that had been involved in drugs and weapons exchanges. Though Joey had never met the man, he had heard others talk of him. Joey did admit to being in the same location at one time during a deal. He couldn't be certain, but he thought he saw the man from a distance.

Mark began to wonder if there was a possibility that Rat Face's boss might be the same as Joey's boss. If he could make that connection and tie the weapons deals and the drug deals together, it could be as simple as one hit to remove the biggest crime lord in the city. As far as he knew.

When he had finished checking trail cameras over the hundreds of acres he made his way back to the house. He made a mental note to review the information from Joey about his contacts and his experiences to see if he could make the connection. That would have to wait because today was supposed to be time with the family. Mark had left early that morning to ensure more daylight hours for him with the kids. Soon Angie would have the picnic lunches packed and they would head for the lake.

"Good morning, sunshine."

Angie's voice was tired but very welcome to Mark's ears. She sat at the small table on the back deck nursing a cup of coffee.

"Good morning. What brings you here this early?"

"I've been packing the picnic basket while you were out and I heard the ATV coming. I thought I might come outside and say hello."

"Well, hello there. Do you need any help packing lunches?" Mark dismounted the four wheeler, almost dropping the small packet of SD cards in his hand.

"No. I finished that a few minutes ago," she said with a smile, "I was going to wake the kids up in a little bit to get them ready to go. Did you have any luck this morning?"

Mark stepped up onto the deck and gestured to her with the small black pouch.

"Well, we'll have a look and see but I think there's some hope." Mark stepped inside the door after a quick kiss and headed toward the computer. He always kept a spare set of cards to swap out when he checked the cameras. That way, he could review what the cameras had caught without worrying that he might miss something else. It had only been a week since he checked the trail cameras before, and it wouldn't take long to review the photographs. Still, it would take time and he really wanted to go to the lake. He decided instead to wake the kids and get on their way. The turkeys could wait.

For most of the day Mark got to enjoy his two most prized things in life: his family, and the outdoors. He spent precious time with his kids, teaching them to fish and hauling in some pretty impressive catches. Angie had insisted on bringing the kayaks along so they got in a little paddle time that afternoon. The picnic lunch was simple but filling and the area they chose was peaceful and quiet. Most of the other people at the lake that day were gathered closer to the boat ramps where there were some grills and picnic tables available, so the area they decided on was almost devoid of others. On occasion a random boat might cruise through or the sounds of a small group might echo along the banks, but for the most part it was rather serene.

The temperature was quite pleasant and the sun was full, prompting Angie to attempt a tan. While Mark busied himself with cleaning up the picnic blanket and putting things away, she slipped out of her shorts and T-shirt and prepared a spot to sunbathe. As he returned from the truck he spotted his bride sprawling out across the beach blanket in a tiny blue two piece bikini.

"Wow," was all he could utter.

"Shut up," she replied with a wry smile.

"That's new…and so…tiny. And…hot! And…"

"Shut up," came the response again. The smile broadened as her face flushed, "You're embarrassing me."

"Embarrass? Well, I do see a lot of bare a..,"

"Shut up!" she smiled widely, "It's not *that* small! And it's actually not new. I bought it last year on sale. I just never had a reason to wear it before today."

"Honey," Mark grinned, "if you *ever* feel the need to wear that again, you just let me know. I'll make up a reason."

Mark stretched out beside her on the ground, trying his best to be helpful and apply suntan lotion wherever she needed it, and a few places she didn't. The kids kept themselves entertained on the bank a few yards away, skipping stones and harassing the local frog population as best they could.

After a few minutes he became totally absorbed in the moment and completely relaxed, smiling as he watched his family. Simple times. Simple activities. No phones. No television. No video games. Simply being together without interruption. He wished he could have this moment all the time. The classic Jim Croce song "Time in a Bottle" popped in his head as he turned his gaze back to his wife. She was more beautiful than ever to him.

"I have got to be the luckiest man on earth," he muttered to himself.

It was a good day.

A week and a half went by with regular, but not daily, efforts to find Rat Face's work shop. Each time Mark followed the man it was pretty much the same route. Until Thursday.

Reduction

Thursday the van swung into the storage facility and he retrieved a box or two, which wasn't uncommon, then he made another stop a few blocks away at a small, nondescript building. Mark hadn't seen him stop there before. The sun was beginning to set as the man quickly moved several boxes from the van into the structure, then locked the van up and disappeared inside.

The look of the building was that of an old convenience store. Probably built in the 1940's, but fairly well maintained. The windows were all covered in paper, so that any chance of seeing what went on inside was out of the question. Mark decided that his best option was to sit and wait for a while to see if Johnson had any contraband when he finally came out. He sent a text to Thompson and informed him of the building and location, then settled in to watch what happened.

Reduction

The neighborhood wasn't bad. Like many others in this part of town, it was older and the architecture reflected its age. The streets were a bit narrower and mostly residential structures dominated each side. There was a new gas station at the end of the block, but other than that there were mostly houses. Mark could imagine that decades earlier the building Johnson was in was probably a small mom and pop general store of sorts. Catering to the immediate needs of the neighborhood, which most likely were local factory workers and their families. Middle class all the way.

About 11:30 that evening, the side door once again opened and Johnson stepped out, quickly producing a set of keys and locking the door behind him. Mark couldn't see any sign of weapon craft or boxes of parts in his hands, so he assumed the man had not finished his work inside quite yet. Now might be a good time to call in the sting. If they could catch

Reduction

him during his next work session, they should have plenty of evidence to nail him on several counts of NFA violation at the least. As Johnson's van pulled away, Mark grabbed his burn phone.

He pressed the SEND button and then began looking the neighborhood over for a hide site he could use to cover the raid. John had wanted him to be their "overwatch," as he called it, and keep an eye out for anything that might complicate the arrest. The problem was that there weren't any lofty positions close by to watch over from. The best he could come up with was parking on the side of the street several hundred yards away and that would not only restrict his view of the entire building, but would not provide an ideal shooting position. There would be no trigger time on this one, even if things went sideways. He simply couldn't risk the exposure.

As soon as John had received the text the ball was in motion to organize a multi-pronged raid on all of the locations Mark had followed the man to. Primarily, they would focus on the workshop and the storage building, but they would also have officers visit the residential locations as well. Dahlgren wanted to take no chances in making sure the sting went off without a hitch.

Since most of the preparations were already made, it was simply a matter of getting the paperwork approved and assembling the teams. Within the week, Dahlgren's men were ready to move on all locations simultaneously. Mark was to position himself down the street from the workshop and observe and report if anything looked out of place.

He hated not being able to take a more active role, but this was not to be his show. To show his appreciation, the Chief had managed to slip a few dollars aside for a "finder's fee" for Mark. He knew how much time it could take to track someone like Johnson down and he appreciated the effort.

Reduction

Mark made his way to the predetermined vantage point and pulled to the curb. It was still early afternoon and Johnson wasn't typically here before 5:00 or so. According to the text from John, the police assets were staging at each location. As soon as Johnson arrived and unlocked the door, all teams would move in and secure all locations. Hopefully, it would all happen without incident and they would have a nice catch for their efforts.

Mark passed the time with a late lunch and gently nursed a large drink. He didn't want his bladder to call on him when he needed to be alert and watching the situation unfold.

Traffic in the area was very light, which made him feel better about collateral damage. The whole time he sat there were only a few vehicles that passed. Of those, only one had actually stopped in the neighborhood. Everything was so quiet, Mark thought about the irony of an arms manufacturer working in the midst of it all.

A few minutes before 5:00 Mark spotted the familiar shape of the van turning the corner at the end of the street. He grabbed the phone and had John's number ready to dial, just in case. As the van pulled in beside the building, Mark slipped his binoculars out of the bag beside him on the seat and watched. There he was, digging feverishly for the keys in his pocket. Totally unaware of what was about to happen. He stepped out of Mark's line of sight to the side door. As he did, something caught Mark's attention on the other side of the street. He focused his gaze on the only car that had stopped earlier. A no frills sedan that could have been anyone's grandmother's car. But it wasn't a grandmother in the front seat. Two men in suits watched the store from the opposite side as Mark. They appeared to be just as interested in Rat Face as he was, maybe more.

Mark tapped the phone and dialed John, "Hey, man, there are a couple of guys in a car across the street and a couple houses up from the building. Are they yours?"

"What kind of vehicle?"

"White sedan. Guys in suits. They yours?"

"Nope. We're moving in now. All my guys are in tactical gear. Keep sharp. Gotta go."

Thompson hung up and within seconds the street was flooded with police vehicles. Mark watched as the tactical teams surrounded the building and spread out. He looked at the sedan. The men inside were surprised at the sudden change of scenery before them and sat staring with mouths agape. One was fumbling with a cell phone as the team made their entrance into the building.

From his position, Mark could hear the verbal exchange at the small store. No gunfire. That was good. He saw movement from the sedan as the duo made their way across the street toward the teams. As they quickly crossed the street their jackets blew open and exposed a pair of sidearms, holstered at the 4 o'clock position on each man.

Mark called John again wanting to desperately let his friend know what was happening.

"Yeah," came the answer. Cursing and ranting clearly audible in the background.

"You got company coming. The two from the sedan are coming up. They have holstered pistols. Head on a swivel, man."

"Got 'em," John said and quickly ended the call.

Mark sat, listening for the sound of gunfire that still never came. He wondered what the men were doing and who they were. After several tense minutes the tactical team withdrew and John emerged with the two men beside him, his phone to his ear.

Reduction

Rat Face was escorted to a nearby cruiser and seated, not so gently, in the back. Crime scene investigators moved in and began to document the scene. Mark wondered what all they had found. His mind raced with thoughts of the inventory this man might have. Well, John would bring him up to speed later. Right now he was tired and just wanted to go home.

His burn phone rang telling him he had a new text. It was from John.

Go home. Will call later. Good job.

With that Mark started the engine and began the drive home. That's when the realization struck him; this was the first job he hadn't pulled a trigger on and was going to get paid for. It felt kind of strange.

Later that night John called to bring him up to speed on the bust. What he told Mark was more than he expected.

"Chief wanted me to thank you again for your help. This was an excellent bust. Your intel really paid off in a big way."

"Glad to help. Did you nab anything good?"

"Well," John began, "at the workshop we caught him with 26 firearms in various stages of modification. Some were being converted to full auto, some to short barrel configurations, some to both. He had a Glock on the table that, for the life of me, I think he was trying to turn into a full auto, like the Model 18 they put out a few years ago. That was crazy. He had all the parts to finish them all up and several more.

"At the residences we didn't find any weapons, but we did find some paperwork that we think will show inventory and transaction information. Maybe we can get some customers and contacts there. His wife is PISSED!" John let a little chuckle slip as he spoke. Apparently, she was unaware of his extra income and just assumed he was working a second part time job at night.

"The storage building was where we found the mother lode," John continued, "The last I heard, the count on disassembled firearms was at 52. Finished goods, already converted or modified, was another 37. The best part? They found four pounds of explosives. I don't mean firecrackers either. This guy actually had military grade high explosives!"

Mark was stunned. This guy was REALLY dangerous.

"You mean this guy had, what is it called in the movies…C-5?"

"No. Not C-4. That's only one type of explosive. This guy actually had some of what's known as Composition B. You get it from *inside* artillery shells. This dude must have some serious connections somewhere."

Reduction

Mark sat silently as his mind grasped as the situation he had helped expose was laid before him.

"Wait, what about the suits? Who were they?"

"You're gonna love this. Those two were ATF agents that had been staking him out also. Chief talked to the local office months ago to see if they would help with the gun running problems we have had amongst the gangs here in town. They brushed it aside and acted like they weren't interested in any kind of joint task force. Then they decided to go out and tackle it on their own without involving us.

"They had actually been selling the guy guns to see what he did and where they went to build a case as well. Kind of like a little version of what the old Fast and Furious program was. They didn't think we'd be able to bust him before they would so they never told us what they were doing.

"They didn't count on us having the one thing they didn't."

"What's that?" Mark asked.

"An out of work machinist with great eyesight and nothing better to do!"

John and Mark both enjoyed a small chuckle at the situation before John turned the attention back to business.

"Say, if you can meet tomorrow I'll see what I can do about getting your salary lined up. Sound good?"

"Sure does. I'll be free all week. I mean, it's not like I have anything better to do." Mark smiled.

Chapter 9

True to his word, Dahlgren sent a nice payment off to Mark for his services. Inside the envelope was a short note thanking him for his aid in the sting and arrest. Typed, not handwritten, and unsigned. No traces.

John eased back in the chair at Mark's workbench.

"You know," he started, "that little rat faced dude was quite the machinist. You'd probably be impressed with some of his work."

"You think so?" Mark smirked.

"Yeah. We got to looking and a lot of the stuff he used to modify was actually made there in that little building. The guy said he used to be an armorer when he was in the military a few years ago. That's where he got his understanding of how things work. Long story short, he got injured and discharged, but couldn't find a job. Through a series of unfortunate events he managed to make contact with the local criminal elements and went to work for them. Some of his stuff has gone across the borders, south and north, and a lot of it has shipped out of state."

"Is that so?" Mark hardly seemed impressed with the tale.

"Check this out," John reached into his pocket and produced a small lever device with a spring that looked like it might have come from a ballpoint pen. He handed it over to Mark.

"OK. What is it?"

"That's called a DIAS. A Drop In Auto Sear. You put that inside of an AR-15 with the right hammer and trigger group and it goes full auto. The ATFE classified those little devices as NFA regulated items years ago. This dude was building them from scratch by the dozen."

Mark studied the small mechanism. The fit and finish was actually pretty good. Too bad the man couldn't put those skills to better use.

"Did you find anything out about his clientele?"

"A few names have popped up, but he hasn't given the big one up yet. We've been trying to negotiate with him on a plea, but he's not willing to budge. He's scared. Maybe we should have let you shoot him in the shoulder."

John's joke didn't go unnoticed.

"That only works with former co-workers. And next time I'm not giving up on the cash either."

Two days later Mark came inside from mowing the lawn and noticed that he had a message on his burn phone.

Cracked the rat. Showtime. Call ASAP.

John must have gotten the name of the main man in the criminal pyramid. He'd want to meet and discuss details and there was no way Mark was going to meet him smelling the way he did at the moment. After all, even an assassin needs to feel fresh for work, right?

After a speedy bath and a change of clothes, Mark called John to get the scoop.

"Where are you at?" The tone in John's voice was urgent.

"Home. Been mowing the yard. What's up?"

"How quick can you meet me?"

"Where?"

"The Red Dot at Columbia and Franklin?"

"Give me 20 minutes. Do I need to bring anything special?"

"Yes. Something you can see a long way with and something you can get in close. Cover the bases."

The phone went dead and Mark rushed to the workshop. He grabbed the bolt action 30-06 and some ammunition and locked the door. On the way to the truck he picked up his trusty 1911 and two spare magazines for it. Soon he was on his way into town.

As he pulled into the parking lot of the convenience store he saw John's Jeep on the opposite side of the lot and moved up along side.

Before he could stop John was out of his vehicle and heading toward Mark's.

"What's up?"

"Hang on, let me get in."

John slid in the passenger side of the truck and buckled up.

"We got a name late last night and some verified information that we need to act on now. As in right now."

"OK. I don't have any time to plan this out?"

Reduction

"Not this time, man. Sorry. I don't think it will be as hard to put together as before though. You already know the area intimately and the target ought to hit you right between the eyes."

Mark's curiosity was through the roof and gaining altitude by the second.

"What do you mean? Am I going back into the east side again?"

"Nope. You're going back to work."

"I know, but where am I going to be working, dude? I need a vantage point and ranges and…"

"The plant. You're going to be shooting from your old place of work. It's ground zero for this one, buddy."

Mark was surprised, to say the least. Who was the target?

"OK. So, who am I shooting and when?"

"You might want to pull over for a second," John said as he pointed to a small parking lot on the right side of the road.

Mark eased the truck to a stop and looked at his friend. Confusion and concern raced through his mind and apparently across his face at the same time.

"Your target will be at the plant this afternoon at around 3:30. The plant is up for sale and he will be showing the property to potential investors. They are supposed to be there around 4:00. That gives you a 30 minute window to take him out."

"Who is it?" For anyone to have access to the plant it would have to either be a realtor or a former executive from the plant.

"James Avery."

"Wait. James P. Avery? As in Chairman of the Board Avery?"

"That's the one. We busted every record in the books to verify his involvement. We even called your old buddy Joey. It seems that Mr. Avery is the one who put him in contact with the men he ended up working for. Avery is heavily invested in the criminal activities of a lot of bad people. He doesn't get his hands directly dirty by dealing, pimping, or trafficking, but he provides a LOT of logistical support and resources. Joey wasn't suspicious because there were several layers of insulation between Avery and the guys he ultimately went to work for."

Mark slumped back in the seat, speechless. Though he had never met Avery he knew who he was and knew his reputation. No doubt that he was one of the first to jump on outsourcing the plant to points across the globe. That man's life revolved around one thing and one thing only: money.

"OK. So, I get into the plant, set up a hasty hide and drop him when he rolls through the gate. Then what?"

Reduction

"I would suggest you park close enough that you can make a quick escape. The interstate is a couple of blocks away, get there and get out. Do you have anything you can take the shot with?"

"I brought the bolt .30-06 and some ammo. It won't be quiet, but it will reach out there. I should be able to hit him from anywhere in that neighborhood if I can catch him out of the car. I'll park on the other side of the railroad tracks around the back side of the plant. It will be close enough I can get in and out quickly."

"Vantage point? Where are you going to take the shot from? I'll try to keep my people away from there if I can."

Mark studied for a minute.

"I think I can get on top of the roof from an old catwalk that maintenance used for the overhead conveyor systems. I know it opens onto the roof, but

I'll have to keep low. I can cover the entire building from there."

"You'd better go. Take me back to the Jeep and I'll start running interference for you. Don't waste any time. It's already 1:30."

Mark looked at the dashboard clock. 1:27. He had to get moving.

After dropping John at his car, Mark made as direct a path to the plant as he could. He surveyed the building as best he could along the front. A railroad service track ran along the back, separating the building from the residential area on the back side and providing his access point. From his years there Mark knew there was a gap in the security fence large enough for him to slip through. He parked his truck, grabbed his bag and began strolling as calmly as he could toward the plant.

He crossed the railroad tracks and found the gap in the fencing. Trying not to draw attention to himself he sat down on the ground beside the fence and surveyed the area. Not a soul was in sight, so he casually slipped through the fence and down the bank on the other side. Soon he was at the receiving dock doors. One of them, he remembered, had a busted lock. He quickly found the door and tried to get in. It wouldn't budge. Someone had fixed the doorknob. His mind raced for options. As he looked around he noticed there was still a trailer backed up to the receiving dock just down from where he stood.

Mark raced along the back wall and quickly stepped up onto the steel bumper of the trailer. Through the crack between the trailer and the padded dock seal he could see the inside of the plant was devoid of life. That would change soon.

He pushed the seal open and slid his bag through followed by his body. It was a tight squeeze, but it worked. He was inside and on his way to the conveyor access way. As he moved he checked the time: 2:12. Within a few minutes Mark was on top of the building and picking a vantage point that covered the entrance and gate.

Avery was known to be a prompt man and hated to be kept waiting himself. No doubt that was why he was unlocking the facility a half hour before anyone else got there.

Mark reached for the ammunition he had brought. He remembered from years gone by that the distance from where he was to the gate was approximately 250 yards. Bobby, the facilities engineering designer, had complete layouts of the plant on all levels and had been tasked once with getting a total square footage for the facility for a financial effort. That included the parking areas, cooling ponds, and guard houses. All that meant that Mark could calculate bullet drop more accurately today. He loaded the first of the sabot rounds into the magazine, followed by the second and third. He

Reduction

figured if he couldn't drop the man with three he needed to quit anyway. The .223 caliber bullets would be shooting extremely fast and flat, so he hoped his bullet drop figures were close enough.

It was now 2:40. Mark's adrenaline was already pumping and he tried to calm himself down. He didn't want to replay his experience with Joey today. Or ever, for that matter.

"It's just a job," he muttered to himself, "Just another job."

Deep breaths helped to calm his nerves a bit and soon he was feeling far less anxious. Time? 3:14. Avery should be here soon.

In the distance Mark could hear the traffic of the interstate. His escape route. The roar of traffic along the roads was constant. Day and night the cars and trucks kept the pavement warm. Gradually, he became aware of a change in the traffic sounds. Less roar and more horns blowing. There was definitely something going on over there. Probably a traffic jam or fender bender. As long as it was clear before he was done, Mark really didn't care.

It was now 3:22 and a new sound grew louder. At first Mark thought it was a train, but then he realized the unmistakable sound of rotor chop. The fender bender must have been much worse as the medevac helicopter from Saint Matthew's circled for a landing zone. Circled. Right above the plant.

"Oh, shit." Mark grabbed the phone again.

"Yeah," John's voice came to life on the other end.

"Got a problem here," Mark announced.

"What's wrong?" John's throat suddenly became as dry as desert sand.

"I've been spotted. Big time."

"What? By who?"

"Medevac. Wreck on the interstate. They flew right over my head looking for a place to park."

Reduction

"Are you sure they saw you?"

"Brother, if they didn't see me, they don't need to be flying that thing. What do you want me to do?"

"Hang tight. Let me check something." John turned on his radio and listened in on the police traffic. A few seconds later he was back on the phone.

"Did they see your face?"

"I don't think so. When I realized what it was I looked away so they couldn't ID me. They had to see me on the roof though. No way they would have missed me laying up here with a rifle."

"Oh, yeah, you've been made, man. Dispatch is sending units now to your location. You got maybe six minutes until cruisers get there. The jam on the interstate will slow some, but not all of them.

"If you get the shot, take it and get the hell out of there. Lose the phone too. You remember."

Reduction

"Got it. Wait, I have a car coming up to the gate now. Gotta go."

Mark flipped open the covers to the Leupold Special Purpose scope and put the stock to his shoulder. The car slowed to a stop at the gate and the driver's side door opened. As the figure stepped out he fumbled for keys to the padlock, finally deciding on one to try. He stepped up to the gate just as another car approached. This was going sideways fast.

Mark eyed the first man and then the new arrival. The second person appeared to be the realtor, with a crest of some sort on his left chest and a sticker on the door of the car. The first man turned as he spoke to the realtor and unlocked the gate.

In the distance Mark could swear he heard sirens. He steadied his breathing and focused on the man in front. The sound of the medevac helicopter's turbines grew louder and louder as it prepared to lift from the nearby accident scene.

Reduction

The helicopter climbed above the street lights and swung around to vector back toward the hospital, crossing line of sight with Mark once again. In his mind he could hear the radio chatter exposing him to the crusaders that were already on their way. He kept his focus on the man in his crosshairs.

Suddenly, Avery looked up at the helicopter almost directly into Mark's scope. Time slowed as Mark recognized the face.

He exhaled slightly and pressed the trigger to the rear. The sound of the 30-06 cartridge was muffled in his ears by the sound of the rotor chop and the throbbing of his own pulse. The .223 bullet peeled out from inside of the plastic sabot and streaked across the property with an almost turbine like whine of its own.

Impact. The round found its mark in the center of Avery's chest. The velocity of the round transferred into the rib cage with devastating cavitation. Avery jerked and slumped forward, hitting his face on the chain link gate as his lungs, pancreas and spleen all shuddered from the violent intrusion. The heart itself was hit almost dead center and practically exploded from the shockwave. The tiny projectile carried on, shedding parts of the copper jacket as it began to tumble into the spinal column, tearing tissue along its path. Avery was dead before he hit the ground.

As Avery was crumpling at the gate, Himes was already breaking down on the run. He stuffed the rifle into the bag and low ran to the roof access doorway. Sirens were clearly audible now. They couldn't be more than a few hundred yards away and were closing fast.

Mark leapt down the final steps of the maintenance stairs and rushed across the plant to the receiving docks again. Finding his entry point he stuffed himself and his bag back through and quickly rushed to the fence. He could hear that the police cruisers had cut their sirens at the front gate and he grabbed the burn phone again.

"Where are you?" John was right to the point.

"Crawling through the fence. What's my situation?"

"Hang on. I'm coming. Play along when I get there."

Mark stood up and began to walk toward his truck that he had parked under an overpass a couple of blocks away. Within a few seconds John was rolling up fast on his left.

"Get in. Hurry."

Mark didn't ask, he just jumped in the passenger side seat and grabbed the buckle, tossing the gear bag in the back as he went.

The Jeep sprang to life as the pair swung around and headed back toward the plant.

"Uh, what are you doing?" Mark asked nervously.

"Follow my lead. And keep your mouth shut."

They rolled right up to the front of the factory and were immediately stopped by one of the officers.

"Sir, you're going to have to leave. This is police business."

John showed him his badge and gestured to the radio in the console.

"It's OK, son. I'm one of you guys. Did you get him yet?

"Sorry, sir. I didn't know. Um, no. We just arrived on scene and haven't secured the area yet." Medevac spotted one man on the roof. Caucasian, red tee shirt and jeans with a rifle. We got the call, but as you know traffic has been a bit of a problem nearby." The officer eyed Mark curiously as he sat there in his red tee shirt and blue jeans.

"OK, son. Do you need anything from me? If not, we're going to go grab a drink. It's my day off, after all."

"Sir, if I might ask; your friend…"

"Mark? Yeah, we've been out assing around all day. Thought we'd go check out that new place for dinner; you know the one where the girls are about half naked? I hear the food is good too." John smiled like a teenager caught coming in past curfew with lipstick smeared across his face.

"He's been with you all day?"

"Well, not all day, no. He had to mow the yard this morning, but I can vouch for him beyond that."

The young officer eyed the pair for a second and then said, "Thank you sir. No, we have this under control. Be sure to let me know how the…menu is." He smiled and returned to the scene.

Reduction

Thompson turned the Jeep around and headed back away from the gate toward Mark's truck.

"Sometime's the best way to hide is right in plain sight," John said, "Now, we need to get the eyes off you a little more.

"Reach in that gym bag back there in the floor. You need a change."

Mark turned and reached into the back of the Jeep, grabbing the bag and hoisting it into his lap.

"Dig in there and get a shirt out. Anything but red."

"Whoa! Man! What are these; cadaver clothes?" The smell nearly made Mark jump out of the Jeep and into the street.

"No, those are my workout clothes. Now, shut up and get a different shirt on. I don't get to do laundry every day, you know."

"What months do you actually wash these?" Mark snurled his nose as he pulled a blue shirt out and slipped it over his head.

"Dude, you stink!"

John just laughed as he turned the corner toward Mark's truck. A line of police cars streamed past as they made the turn. Mark and John exchanged glances.

"So, what do you say we check out that new place after all?"

Mark looked over his shoulder at the cars now in the distance.

"I think that sounds like a fine idea to me."

Reduction

Epilogue

Mark never asked how Dahlgren was able to move the money around, but was pretty happy he did. Thanks to some financial manipulation, he now had a regular salary instead of a commission. It wasn't much, but he was "officially" on the payroll as a maintenance man for the department. Dahlgren had also promised that, if he was ever called on again to take care of any "varmint problems," he would be compensated in addition to his regular pay. Off the record, of course.

From time to time he picked up an occasional machining project, which he thoroughly enjoyed. It kept his skills sharp and gave him an excuse to get away to the workshop for a while. There, tucked away from prying eyes, was a special tool box full of his various tools and accessories he had developed in secret, along with a tiny device that looked a lot like some sort of lever with a spring from a ballpoint pen.

Mark appreciated the accommodations made for him, but still wanted to get back into an actual, legal profession. One that didn't shoot back or get him arrested would be nice. So, he sat in his recliner scanning the help wanted ads of the local paper, hoping his skills would match someone's needs.

Then his phone rang.

ALSO FROM BRIAN CHEATHAM

FURTHER REDUCTION

ISBN: 978-1-976-46826-1

Book #2 of the Reduction Saga

When the economy turned bad Mark Himes was offered an opportunity he never anticipated: use his skills as a hunter to reduce crime in his city. Operating outside the law, but under the direction of the Chief of Police, he has helped eliminate some of the department's most successful criminals. Now, he is not alone.

A vigilante is on the loose, making Mark an even bigger target than he was. The Chief has ordered Himes to find and stop this new factor before innocent people get caught in the crossfire. Since his operations are closely guarded secrets, he himself is on the most wanted list.

Let the deadly game of cat and mouse begin.

Made in the USA
Columbia, SC
04 September 2018